SABINE DURRANT

Ooh
la la!
Connie
Pickles

PUFFIN

PUFFIN BOOKS

Published by the Penguin Group
Penguin Books Ltd, 80 Strand, London WC2R 0RL, England
Penguin Group (USA) Inc., 375 Hudson Street, New York, New York 10014, USA
Penguin Group (Canada), 90 Eglinton Avenue East, Suite 700, Toronto, Ontario, Canada M4P 2Y3
(a division of Pearson Penguin Canada Inc.)
Penguin Ireland, 25 St Stephen's Green, Dublin 2, Ireland (a division of Penguin Books Ltd)
Penguin Group (Australia), 250 Camberwell Road, Camberwell, Victoria 3124, Australia
(a division of Pearson Australia Group Pty Ltd)
Penguin Books India Pvt Ltd, 11 Community Centre, Panchsheel Park,
New Delhi – 110 017, India
Penguin Group (NZ), 67 Apollo Drive, Rosedale, North Shore 0632, New Zealand
(a division of Pearson New Zealand Ltd)
Penguin Books (South Africa) (Pty) Ltd, 24 Sturdee Avenue, Rosebank,
Johannesburg 2196, South Africa

Penguin Books Ltd, Registered Offices: 80 Strand, London WC2R 0RL, England

puffinbooks.com

First published 2007
3

Text copyright © Sabine Durrant, 2007
All rights reserved

The moral right of the author has been asserted

Set in 12/15 pt Joanna by Palimpsest Book Production Limited, Grangemouth, Stirlingshire
Made and printed in England by Clays Ltd, St Ives plc

British Library Cataloguing in Publication Data
A CIP catalogue record for this book is available from the British Library

ISBN: 978-0-141-31941-4

To the Smiths

Chapter One

New vocab: un quai (platform); ne pas manquer (to be in time for); faire foirer quelque chose (to mess something up)

Friday 28 March
❤ *Eurostar, carriage sixteen, pulling out of Waterloo, 9.10 a.m.*

I think I can honestly say this is the most exciting moment of my life.

Julie, who is reading over my shoulder, says that I'm a tragic human being and that the most exciting moment of her life was halfway through Wednesday night when she met Karl. This is what I say:

1. Karl wears red trousers and she once told me never to trust a boy who wore red trousers.

2. I bet he only lasts two minutes. None of her boyfriends lasts longer than that.

3. She should keep her big nose out of my diary.

[Squiggles on page due to undignified scuffle.]

Now I have my pen back. (It's a lovely thin-nibbed Pentel.) OK, they weren't red, they were 'wine-khaki'. And OK, she hasn't got a big nose. Just medium.

She's listening to her iPod now, staring out of the window with a lovesick expression on her face, so I've got a few minutes' peace.

Oh! I can't believe I'm finally on my way. I'm always telling everyone that Paris is my natural home, and now's my chance to prove it. I know it's only two and a bit weeks and that it's only a French exchange, but I feel in my bones that something important is going to happen. I'm going to be *as one* with the French way of life. I may look embarrassingly English now — thick tights and floral frock from Oxfam are a mistake and I've made my skin blotchy picking those spots on my chin — but in two weeks I will be a changed person. I will be chic. I will be *soignée*. I will be pimple-free. I will probably wear black.

Hang on, there goes Julie's phone. It's Monsieur Baker. We got separated from him and the rest of the group in Departures. It was so chaotic, what with Cyril and Marie, my half-brother and half-sister, charging around, and Mother all teary and William and Delilah . . . but I'm not going to think about that now . . . and what with Karl being there in his red – I mean wine-khaki – trousers, that by the time we got through Passports I was a limp rag. Julie yanked me into WHSmith to buy a copy of *Elle* and some cigarettes and I let the situation slip. (Honestly, I don't know why someone as prim as me is best friends with Julie. Or vice versa.) The queue was ridiculous and by the time she'd paid and slotted her Marlboro Lights into the back pocket of her jeans – some feat of engineering considering how tight they are – the others had disappeared up the moving escalator.

There was a drunken man taking his trousers off and trying to have a pee at the bottom so the ticket collector was a bit distracted and we fanned our passports and ran through. The train was already making noises and I had to yell at Julie to run – she's wearing wedge espadrilles (honestly, in this weather!) and her boobs were bouncing up and down in her stripy halter-neck.

'Hurry up!' I shouted. 'We can't miss the train. Paris awaits!'

She couldn't breathe when she finally sat down. Turns out you can't smoke on the train anyway. Good thing too. I love Julie for all her faults, and I don't want her to die of lung cancer before she's even lost her virginity.

I am slightly concerned about the others. I was all for going to join them in carriage eighteen about five minutes ago, but Julie says Monsieur B will come and find us if he's that bothered. Now she's nodded off to sleep with her mouth against the window and I don't have the heart to wake her.

I've just reread the details of my French exchange student.

Name: *Pascale Blanc*
Family: *Father (hotel supplier); Mother (housewife); two brothers (older)*
Hobbies: *Fashion, rock music, literature*

She sounds intriguing and I like her handwriting on the form. Her family sounds tidy and grown-up too. Just the sort of thing I like. Mine's so higgledy-piggledy, what with my own father being dead and Jack, my stepfather, being divorced from my mother, and Marie and Cyril being so irritatingly little. Sometimes I think I'm the only person who keeps everything together. A conventional family with older siblings will be restful. I'm not so sure about Pascale's hobbies. Julie says it's about time I took some interest in fashion and rock music. My personal style is what I like to call 'charity-shop chic', i.e. anything I can find that's wacky and cheap. Julie thinks I need to be a bit more Miss Selfridge and a bit less Dr Barnado's. I'm so glad Pascale likes literature. I've started reading *Madame Bovary*, which is quite hard work. Pascale's probably read it several times and I expect we'll discuss it late into the night.

❤ Eurostar, train track in the French countryside, 11.50 a.m.

I went to sleep. It must have been the rhythm of the train. It seems to be running faster and smoother this side of the Channel. Of course it does; everything is better here. Julie's still snoring next to me. I can't believe I missed the tunnel. I'm actually in France! The landscape is beautiful. Flatter than I'd imagined – dark furrowed fields stretching out like giant rumpled handkerchiefs under the lowering dark sky. (Sorry: I must stop trying to be too poetic. It's just showing off.) A church with a steeple in the distance. And walking along that road a man with a dog in a beret. The man's in the beret, I mean, not the dog.

The countryside is turning into town – tall buildings, pavements, cars. There's something beautiful about the shape of French houses – the steep pitch of the roofs, the golden colour of the brickwork, the shutters, the wrought-iron balconies. Those houses there are just *so* French. You couldn't find them anywhere else.

We've made good time. We must be getting into Paris. It's strange that Monsieur Baker hasn't come to look for us. I expect we'll meet him on the platform. I can't see anything I recognize from pictures yet, like Sacré Cœur, or the Eiffel Tower. It looks more industrial than I'd thought. And — stupid, I know — I hadn't imagined it to be drizzling.

We're slowing down. Julie's stirring. In a few minutes my feet will be on real French soil. I'm going to remember this moment for the rest of my life. France, oh France.

❤ *Belgium, 12.25 p.m.*

Oh God.

Chapter Two

New vocab: un *embouteillage* (a traffic jam); une *zone industrielle* (an industrial estate); une *goth* (a goth)

💜 *Station office, Gare du Midi, Brussels, 12.30 p.m.*

Julie is talking to Monsieur Baker on her phone. I think he is angry — very, very angry. I can tell this by the fact that she has let her hair fall forward to cover her face and that she hasn't looked up to stick her tongue out at me once. A thin man in uniform, also very angry, is talking at us fast and furiously, with lots of hand gestures, but I don't understand because I seem to have forgotten any French I ever knew. Actually, maybe he is speaking that other language they have in Belgium. What is it? Flemish.

It is only just sinking in. We are not in Paris. We are

not even in France. We are miles from France. I wish I'd paid more attention in Geog because then I'd know how many miles.

To be honest, I'm not even sure where Belgium is.

💜 A *taxi in the back streets of Brussels,*
2 p.m.

The station master, or *monsieur de gare* or whatever he's called, became much nicer when he'd calmed down. He said we must have been led on to the wrong platform. It was bad luck that the Brussels train had been delayed. He let us sit in his office while he spoke for a long time on the phone to Monsieur Baker. When he hung up, he wrung his hands and raised his eyes to the ceiling as if to say, 'Whoa, that's one cross French teacher,' which I thought was very human of him.

He gave us a really horrible cup of coffee and then he put us in the taxi that is at this very minute taking us to a coach station. We don't have to pay. Monsieur Baker has sorted that out, though we will have to pay him back. (I feel very bad about Mother.)

We're stuck in traffic. Julie is texting Karl. There's nothing outside the window to fill the heart with glee. The buildings are modern and aloof. Rain streaks the concrete black. The station master says there's a square near by where there's a statue of a little boy peeing. I think it would remind me of my little brother, Cyril, who always leaves the seat wet but whom I'm beginning to miss more than I can say. I feel homesick. Actually maybe I just feel carsick.

❤ A *coach somewhere in Belgium, seat twenty-three, 4.45 p.m.*

Thank goodness we got on this bus. The last one was full. Julie and I sat in a cafe and drank a gallon of Coke, two sandwiches filled with stringy ham, and about eight packaged cakes. Our landlord, John Spence, who is also Mother's boyfriend (but that's another story), gave me fifty euros as a present and I spent eighteen of them on snacks.

Julie has been talking a lot about Karl. He goes to the same school as her last boyfriend, Ade. 'But,' she said, 'he's not the sort of person to get off with someone else when you're in the same room.'

'No.'

We both sat thoughtfully, remembering a fateful party in which Ade had done just that.

'Karl's perfect,' she breathed.

'But he does wear red trousers,' I added.

❤ *Same coach somewhere in France, seat twenty-two, 6.30 p.m.*

I've swapped seats with Julie so as to be by the window. We've crossed the border: lines of poplars, more huge fields, motorways, factories. We might not be seeing France's best side.

Julie has just suggested we make lists of all the boys we've ever fancied. I've humoured her for a bit, but only on the condition we play I spy in French to practise our vocab.

She's just texting Karl – AGAIN – and then she will.

Bother. I can't stop thinking about William now. It *was* odd of him and Delilah to come and say goodbye. Delilah is my next-door neighbour and a good friend – though I don't always like her, if you know what I mean. She was wearing an acid-green mac cinched in at the waist and quite a lot of make-up for so early on a Friday morning. I think she'd really come because she was peed *she* wasn't going on a French exchange (they don't do them at her school – too posh) but she wanted to show me she wasn't.

She said airily, 'We're going on a day trip; William's taking me to Brighton. Thought we'd wave you off as we were passing.'

I tried to catch William's eye but he was scuffing his feet back and forth across the floor as if there was a stain he was trying to clear up. Truth be told, his jeans are so wide and flapping he was in fact mopping clean a small area without realizing.

Things have been a little strange between us since the incident. I keep telling myself it was just a kiss and he wasn't even going out with Delilah when it happened, and it is DEFINITELY for the best that we are just friends.

He looked up, finally, and saw me watching. 'We'll miss ya,' he said casually.

'Me too,' I said.

We gazed at each other. And, for a moment, I forgot all the noise and bustle of Waterloo around me. I just saw my dear friend William – that sweet, sheepish smile he has when he bites the corner of his lip as if trying to stop himself. For a moment I thought there was something still between us, but ... But then Delilah came up and gave him a side-on hug.

Right, I'm going to read *Madame Bovary* now. So far it seems to be about an unhappily married woman who is obsessed with love. Not a good life path. One thing I'm going to do on this trip is flush William from my system. That sounds a bit lavatorial. I should say purge him from my being. Oh dear, that does too. What I mean is: FORGET HIM.

(I've had a horrible thought. Do you think they've done it?)

❤ *Coach in outskirts of Paris, back in seat twenty-three, 7.40 p.m.*

Had to swap seats back as Julie is feeling sick. We are entering Paris through the back door. The coach is going to drop us somewhere near Disneyland (the indignity), where Monsieur Baker will 'hand us over' to our families. I'm beginning to feel nervous. Julie says she'll run away if she doesn't like hers.

We are turning off the motorway so we must be

getting near. We're pulling into an industrial estate. I can see Monsieur Baker waiting with a group of people. On one side of him is a smiley girl in jeans, younger than us, a chubby woman in a tracksuit and several young children in grubby anoraks. On the other is a small woman in a beige raincoat and an angry-looking goth in head-to-toe black. We've come to a halt. I wonder which is mine. Julie has just squeezed my hand. I think I can bear anything except perhaps the goth.

❤ The cleanest bathroom in the world, 9 p.m.

I got the goth.

I'm so tired I can hardly lift my pen. I'm in the bathroom. They think I'm cleaning my teeth.

I almost cried saying goodbye to Julie. She whispered, 'Mine looks about ten and yours looks about twenty-five; do you think they've got us muddled?' as we hugged. I gave her an affectionate whack in the ribs with my elbow so the last I saw of her face was it contorted in fake agony. Oh, I'm going to miss her.

This is stupid, and I'm going to get over it, but I feel lonely. The house is modern and clean, in a cul-de-sac next to other identical houses. There's a tiny old-fashioned kitchen and a big room divided into a sitting area and a dining area, with a massive flat-screen television blaring from the wall. The floors are all cold and tiled. Upstairs, where the bedrooms are, the carpet is dark green and scratchy. It's nowhere near the centre of Paris. We're way out in the suburbs.

Madame de Blanc is like a little brown mouse (complete with whiskers: oh that's so mean, sorry). She's slightly bent and her hair is tied back in a frail bun. No make-up, beige clothes. I keep worrying I'm going to tread on her. I think she wants to be called 'Madame Blanc' because she didn't correct me when I did. One of the side effects of an unconventional upbringing is that you can be a bit free and easy with first names. No sign of Monsieur Blanc or either of Pascale's brothers. You know how other people's houses always smell different, though there's normally food and washing powder involved? Well, this one smells sterile, like my doctor's waiting room.

Pascale does look about twenty-five. Huge black boots, buckles all over her trousers, dyed purple hair, loads of eyeliner. She's pretending she's not interested in me to be cool. At least, I hope she's pretending. She didn't talk to me at all in the car. I tried to chat, but my dictionary was in my rucksack and my French, despite the I spy, has deserted me.

I'm sleeping on a spare bed in her bedroom. The room's covered in posters of snarling pop stars and she's written things in angry felt-tip all over the mirror. The windows are covered in black paper. I've got a drawer for my clothes. At the back, I found a key ring in the shape of a skull.

I rang Mother to tell her I was here safely. She's received a running commentary on our day from Monsieur Baker and has been ver' ver' ver' worried (she often says things in threes). I had to pretend to be ver' ver' ver' jolly to cheer her up. Marie came on and told me all about the Easter Bonnet parade she'd had at school and then I spoke to Cyril – he'd lost his Superhero Top Trumps and I remembered they were on top of the toaster. Now I feel so homesick I can't write any more.

Chapter Three

New vocab: *la banlieue* (the suburbs); *voler à l'étalage* (to shoplift)

Saturday 29 March
♥ *Pascale's bedroom, 1 p.m.*

Some observations:

1. In France you drink hot chocolate from a bowl not a cup.
2. Madame Blanc enjoys cleaning.
3. Pascale snores.

I woke up this morning feeling much more positive. Pascale was still asleep (see observation three, above) but I could hear noises out in the street — voices and birdsong. I lay on the bed, thinking about my long-lost grandparents, the deliciously named Bellechasses. Mother hasn't spoken to her parents for years – they disowned her when she ran off with my poor dead father – but she wrote to let them know I was coming. It is strange they didn't ring when they got her letter. It was only a week ago – I joined the French exchange programme at the last minute. Maybe it hasn't reached them yet.

Madame Blanc, wearing rubber gloves (see observation two), came into the room as I was reading my book, shook Pascale awake and told her to get up, have breakfast (see observation one) and take me for a walk. It wasn't that smooth a negotiation. There was a lot of shouting from Pascale and at one point she threw herself into the bathroom and locked the door. But in the end the two of us left the house together, so you have to assume she agreed.

Once out, she marched off down the road, with me following behind, until we got to a square with a small market. Despite Pascale's unfriendliness I felt a surge of excitement. It looked so colourful: stalls with piles of cheese and salami; red and white striped awnings; a *boulangerie* bristling with bread. The sun had been going in and out, but it felt warm for a moment. The pearl-white buildings turned silver. I would have skipped if it weren't for the look of venom shot my way by Pascale. (Actually she's right: skipping at my age – not a good look.)

She wandered idly past a few stalls selling T-shirts and peasant skirts, pausing only to rifle through a basket of sale items, and then went out the other side, across the road past something called an *auto-école* and into a main shopping street. She went into the *pharmacie*. Rather feebly I followed. It smelt tangy and medicinal, like the stuff Delilah put on her ears after she'd had them pierced, or like some skin-explodingly expensive face cream.

Pascale stood by the make-up counter and tried on a black lipstick.

'Nice,' I said in English. 'Maybe a bit on the dark side?'

She scowled and dusted on some powder.

I started looking at the soaps and a few minutes later realized she'd left the shop.

She was heading back up the main road the way we'd come. Just before we got to the square she went into something called HyperCasino, which was like a small mall with piped music and a supermarket at one end. I ran to catch up with her. She was flicking through a rail of embroidered kaftans.

'Do you think we might go into Paris later?' I said. My oral French isn't bad – I'm in the top set at school and Mother has talked to me in French all my life. My written French is rubbish, which is why I'm writing everything here in English.

She shrugged. Her shoulder bag – army surplus with lots of graffiti in black pen – seemed to be prodding into me.

'Do you go into Paris often?'

She shrugged again and moved off, past the small shops, through a door and back out on to the street.

'Is it far to Paris?'

She tutted and walked even faster. She was heading in the direction of home now. I stopped trying to keep up and trailed behind, feeling stupid and embarrassed. When I reached the house, she was standing on the doorstep being yelled at by a big man in a suit with a neatly cropped beard and small oval glasses. I couldn't understand what he was saying, but he had hold of her khaki shoulder bag and was pulling items out.

'This?' he was saying. 'And this? And this?'

I recognized a slashed top she'd held against herself briefly in the market, and a black jumper I'd seen her look at in the mall, and the black lipstick from the chemist. I didn't remember her paying for any of them.

She saw me coming up and gabbled something shrilly. The man, who, I realized, must be her father, Monsieur Blanc, turned to me and said in perfect English, 'Constance, nice to meet you. But is it correct? Pascale does not have the money. Is it true that you have purchased these items as gifts for her?'

She was glaring at me. I was so cross with her I wanted to land her in it, but I also saw a chance to be her friend. 'Yes, I did,' I said. 'I wanted to give something to Pascale to thank her for having me.'

Monsieur Blanc rubbed his hand over his face wearily. Then he jerked his chin at Pascale. 'OK,' he said. 'Inside.'

Madame Blanc was standing in the hallway in her rubber gloves, looking flustered. Pascale and I went past her and came upstairs to Pascale's room.

'You can thank me if you like,' I said when she'd opened her cupboard to reveal a mirror and started trying on her new top. I got my French dictionary out from my rucksack and flicked through. 'I don't like lying much.'

'My father doesn't like me,' she said. 'He only likes Philippe, my brother.'

'I'm sure he does like you,' I told her. And, with the help of my French dictionary, I said, 'At least you've got one. Mine was killed when I was little. A motorbike accident. He was delivering pizzas.'

'Oh, that's so sad,' she said, sitting down on her bed. After that, I managed to ask her – doing an imitation of her stalking down the road – why she had been so horrible to me. And she managed to tell me that she hadn't wanted an English exchange, that her father had made her because her grades were so bad last term. She said she didn't think we had much in common. 'Your clothes,' she said, wincing, 'are bizarre.'

I said, 'Literature?' She said she'd put that on the end of the form because her teacher had made her.

I said, '*Madame Bovary*?' and she said, 'Madame who?'

'Oh,' I said sadly.

I asked her where her father had been, and she said away on business. He supplies furniture to hotels, which involves a lot of travel. Pascale told me one of her brothers, the youngest, is on a school trip to the Dordogne – back next weekend; the other, the eldest, had been at a friend's for the night and would be home later today.

'Didier – the eldest – is dull,' she said. 'But Philippe you will love. Everyone loves Philippe.'

I told her all about how my mother was French, and explained a bit about my grandparents, thinking that she might be able to help me track them down.

I got the piece of paper with their address on out of my pocket and showed it to her. She widened her eyes and whistled. She said it was a chic *arrondissement*. She said she'd take me after lunch. I don't know if I'll be able to eat anything now. I feel sick with anticipation.

'And do you have a boyfriend?' she asked as we were about to go downstairs.

I began to tell her about William: how he's a really good friend and how we did kiss once by accident but that I blew it by running away and that he's now going out with my next-door neighbour . . . but my French began to go all wonky and so I finished quickly and just said, 'So, no. No. You?'

She has apparently. He's called Eric and he's already left school, but her parents don't like him. 'You'll see him tonight at the party,' she said.

What party?

❤ *Bathroom, 6 p.m.*

Quick update while Pascale is putting on her make-up for tonight.

After I'd written the above we went down for lunch. Monsieur Blanc was sitting at one end of the table, reading his paper. Madame Blanc was sitting cowed and downtrodden at the other. The television was on – showing some news programme – and she got up at one point to switch it off. Monsieur Blanc snapped at her and she switched it back on. The atmosphere after this was tense. We ate: steak; fried potatoes; salad – served one after another in a row. Monsieur B asked me questions in perfect, very precise English. Madame B, who doesn't seem to speak a word of English, did all the serving and clearing. I often think how nice it would be if Mother stayed at home and didn't have to work, but I don't think she'd like a life like Madame B's. Monsieur B didn't help with the washing-up. I think he's that sort of man.

I've smiled so much today my face aches. It's exhausting being a guest in a strange family's home. I'm not sure I'll ever feel relaxed around the Blancs.

After lunch Pascale and I set off for Paris. We walked to the RER, which is like a suburban train. It's ten stops to Châtelet-Les Halles and it takes twenty-five minutes. At first you're above ground – you see lots of houses with shutters, and shops and cars (small cars, not all those horrible four-wheel drives you get in London), but once you're at Nation it goes underground and dark. You feel like you're burrowing into the city like a mouse. Châtelet-Les Halles, this dark, scary underground concourse, is full of lots of other mice, all going in different directions.

I'd have turned round and gone back the way I'd come if I hadn't been with P – I had to run to keep up but at least she knew where she was going. We pushed our way through the throng, through some barriers, and down to another platform where we got Line 4, which is plum-coloured, to Saint-Germain-des-Prés. There were fewer people here, like an ordinary tube station. We got the escalator up into the open air and – there! – my first view of Paris. Beautiful, tall grey-white buildings with wrought-iron balconies, cobbled streets and pavements, mopeds driven by men in suits, red geraniums in pots, chic shops, chic women, a lovely church with a garden, dogs on leads, high heels, pigeons, cafes . . .

Pascale set off down a road with Dior on the corner but stopped halfway down to enter a smart jewellery shop. We both had a browse and when we came out she collared a tall, thin man with a tiny dog – a bit like a poodle, only smaller and fluffier. He gave us directions to my grandparents' apartment while the dog sniffed my trousers. (I'm sure I've washed them since I bought them in Cancer Research.) The dog yapped as we set off and when I turned round the man was still looking at us. I suppose we were a funny sight, Pascale in her goth black and buckles, me in my charity-shop men's trousers. Mind you, a man with that small a canine companion looks a bit odd himself. Cultural observation: in London, people are more size-conscious when it comes to dogs.

We left the main road and wandered down a few side streets – all equally Parisian and gorgeous – until we were standing outside a large, smart white-stone building with a striped awning over the porch.

'*Voilà!*' said Pascale. I grabbed her and pulled her over to the wall. There was a man in uniform standing by the main entrance.

'Oh my God,' I breathed. '*Mon Dieu*, I mean. I'm so nervous.'

She shrugged and said, 'Well, let's leave,' but I said no, that now I was here I wanted to do it. So, I went up to the man, plucked up my courage, and said, '*Bonjour. Je cherche Madame et Monsieur de Bellechasse.*'

He said, '*Pardon?*'

At which point Pascale intervened and started gabbling away far too fast for me. I think she might have been telling him about my mother and my whole story because at one point he lowered the sides of his mouth, and when a motorbike screeched past they both winced. Anyway, at the end of it he said something that I could tell wasn't very hopeful by the accompanying shrug and Pascale said: 'They're not here.'

I must have looked as shattered as I felt because the concierge said in English, 'I am sorry.'

I felt really tired suddenly – the exhaustion of travelling to Belgium and back and all the smiling since seemed to catch me up at the back of my legs. I would have just gone straight back to Pascale's house if she hadn't pulled a notebook and a pen out of her shoulder bag and they both hadn't just stood there watching me.

In the end I wrote the note in English.

Dear Madame and Monsieur de Bellechasse,

You don't know me, but I am Constance your granddaughter. My mother is Bernadette who you haven't seen for all these years. She wrote to you recently, but you never contacted us. I am in Paris for a fortnight, staying with my French exchange family in La Varenne. Their phone number is: 42.88.56.01. I am fourteen. I would love to meet you while I am here.

Yours truly,

Constance (Pickles)

PS You may have heard my father is dead. Mother married again and had Cyril and Marie. Unfortunately she is now divorced. Please don't be cross.

We came straight back here after that. I felt too tired and tearful to do any sightseeing and Pascale was twitchy about getting ready for tonight's party, which I still don't know much about.

Her eldest brother Didier was in the house when we got home. He's got glasses — little ones with no rims — and hair you only see in those pictures in old-fashioned barber shops, almost impossibly neat. Clear complexion, full lips, triangular brown eyes rather like a dog's, and a surprisingly deep voice. He shook my hand and said, 'How do you do?' in English when we were introduced. Monsieur Blanc was being irritable with Madame Blanc for having thrown away a newspaper or something and I saw Didier put his arm round her in the kitchen, whisper in her ear and help her go through the bins.

Later, when we were having a snack (some little fruit tarts from the *boulangerie*), he said to me, 'So, you haven't met Philippe?'

I said no.

'Philippe you will love,' he said.

Isn't it funny how nothing is more likely to put you off someone than people telling you you'll like them?

So, now there's this party to go to. I'm not sure I want to go. But I am sure I don't want to stay behind with Pascale's parents. I feel embarrassed and tense just being in the room with them. I wonder when my grandparents will ring. I wish I could see Julie. She'd tell me to go to this party, wouldn't she? Pascale is out of the bathroom. She's wearing a necklace — a purple cross on a thick gold chain. I could swear we saw it in that shop we went into today.

I will go to this party. I will be poised. I will be mysterious. I will be the cool, detached English girl who everybody wants to meet. I will be the ambassadress of London.

Chapter Four

New vocab: *se peloter* (to get off with each other)

Sunday 30 March

💜 *My bed in Pascale's bedroom, 11 a.m.*

Err. Agh. Blughhhhh. What exactly is Pernod?

💜 *Still my bed, 11.15 a.m.*

Oh God. The events of last night are beginning to unfurl in my head. I can never show my face in La Varenne again.

💜 *Kitchen, 12 noon*

I've staggered downstairs into the pristine kitchen, where I am humming to conjure the illusion that I am on top of the world (as opposed to squashed underneath it). I have gagged my way through a bowl of hot chocolate and am now picking at a piece of dry baguette. Madame and Monsieur are at church. Didier is opposite me at the table reading a book called *Sartre et l'existentialisme* and keeps shooting me amused glances over the top of it.

We didn't go straight to the party. We got a bus and went to a bar where Pascale met up with lots of girls and boys she knew. Someone handed me some Pernod, which tasted disgusting like liquorice, but which I sipped to keep my hands busy. No one talked to me, but they stared a lot. One of the girls – in tight stone-washed jeans and a matching denim jacket – kept looking at me and laughing like a fly trapped under a glass. Pascale and Eric, who has greasy black hair, wears leathers and looks about eighteen, played baby-foot. I stood next to them trying to look interesting. I was hoping there would be people from Pascale's school and there might be some kids from Woodvale with them, but there weren't. They all seemed a bit older.

Finally we left the bar. To my horror, Pascale got on to the back of Eric's motorbike and roared off, leaving me to mill on to a bus with the others. It all started seeming a bit surreal. A boy in shorts and sneakers sat next to me, taking up all the room with his legs wide apart, and asked me questions very loudly, then shouted to his friends over my answers. Luckily quite soon every-body started crowding to the door and we got off. There was a little alley and down the end of it was a sort of scout hut, from which came the sounds of a party. Inside was a jukebox and a table covered in bottles of beer, and a lot of people dancing. Pascale was sitting on Eric's knee at a table in the corner and when I went up she said something to make the others laugh. She wasn't an ally any more. It stopped feeling like an adventure. I was wearing a dress I had found in Trinity Hospice – red and white polka-dot satin – with some purple tights and the shoes Julie calls my lesbian lace-ups. Before we left, I'd thought I looked Bohemian, but now I was here, with everybody else in jeans and polo shirts, I felt like a child in fancy dress who'd wandered into the wrong party.

I left Pascale's table and went over to the table where the drinks were. A boy who'd been one of the most energetic dancers came over to me. He had an interesting face: a cross between an axe murderer and a teddy bear. He was dripping with sweat and his T-shirt was cut off so you could see the hair under his arms. He started trying to make conversation – which was hard over the music and without my dictionary – and was pouring me more of that gross Pernod stuff. He was called François. I was trying to be all poised and ambassadress-like, telling him about Woodvale and my plans for GCSE, but the more I sipped, the more the sound in the room began swirling in my ears, and the bodies gyrating looked like strobes and I couldn't concentrate. The next thing I knew I was on the dance floor and François was prodding the air above me and yanking my arms up and down until I started giggling and thought I was

going to fall over. In fact I did fall over and François
gathered me up and put his tongue in my mouth.

It took me a few minutes to come to my senses and
pull away. It was technically my third kiss and maybe
because of the Pernod I am prepared to give it seven
and a half out of ten.

Previous scores

That boy at the youth club last summer: 5/10
William two weeks ago: 8/10 (would have been
higher but points taken off for embarrassment)

'Merci,' I said, smiling politely, in the manner of an
ambassadress. I meant 'merci for picking me up off the
floor' but François seemed to think I meant 'merci for
kissing me', because he lunged at me and did it again.
This time I said, 'Non, non, non,' – a firm ambassadress – and
went over to the wall. I slightly misjudged it and banged
my shoulder (bruise this morning). François followed
and tried to do it again.

Two girls from the bar were looking at me and
laughing. I said, 'You could help me if you like!' but
they turned away. Honestly, Snootsville. What I could
have done with Julie being there. Or Delilah. *Anyone*.

'So, you want to go outside? Yes?' François said.

'No,' I said. 'I do not want to go outside.' He kept
putting his arm round my waist and trying to pull me
towards him. His eyes were closed.

'Non! Non,' I said. Then I gave in for a bit.

'OK,' I said finally. 'Non.' And pushed him away from me. 'I've got to go.'

I got across the room to where Pascale and Eric were getting cosy in the corner. I tried to convince her to come home with me, but she just looked irritated. I could feel François hovering at my shoulder and I tried making eyes of appeal at her, but she didn't get it. She just kept burying her face back into Eric's. God, it was frustrating. I know some people think I'm uptight, but there is a time and a place and I don't think snogging your greasy-haired, spotty boyfriend when your guest, who's only been in the country five minutes, is having a CRISIS is one or the other.

'Fine!' I said and turned round. Bump. François. In my face again.

'Look,' I said. 'I really like you, but I'm tired. It's really, really late.' I mimed looking at my watch, though I wasn't wearing one. 'I need to go home.'

He nodded and disappeared off. Phew. Then he was back, shrugging on a denim jacket. 'OK. We go,' he said.

'No. No. I have to go. Alone. You stay.'

He smiled at me. '*Chez* Pascale, yes? I take you?'

I gave up. I didn't know where I was going anyway. 'All right. *D'accord*. But no kissing.'

'What?'

'No . . .' I pursed my mouth into a kiss-shape to show him what I meant.

'Ah.' He kissed me again. Everyone was watching.

'No!' I pushed him off. 'None of that. OK?'

He shrugged. 'OK.'

So, he walked me home. It took about forty-five minutes – I was very glad to be wearing my lesbian lace-ups. I think he got a bit fed up about halfway there, but I just kept chattering away in English, pretending he could understand. When we got to the house, I said, '*Merci beaucoup,*' put my hands on his shoulders and kissed him on both cheeks.

The light was on in the living room so I tapped on the front door and Didier opened it. He raised his eyebrows when he saw François and they exchanged a few words which I didn't understand. I felt rather dizzy in the bright light. François, who looked much younger next to Didier, turned and went up the path to the street and I went into the kitchen and got myself a glass of water.

I met Didier as I came out.

'You have already made friends,' he said, with a tight smile.

I laughed as gaily as I could, leaning against the banister for support. 'Yes. Yes,' I said. 'Everyone is so friendly.'

'And Pascale, where is she?'

'She is still out. I expect she'll be back soon.'

Didier frowned.

'I'm fine,' I said. 'I'm fine. Good night.' He didn't answer and I went upstairs. On the last step, I tripped and, when I turned to check he hadn't seen, he was watching me with a funny smile on his face. He's doing it over his bloody book now. God, I could die of embarrassment. I thought I quite liked him, but I don't. He's so patronizing. He must think I've never drunk Pernod before. He must think I'm about six.

❤ *My bed, 4 p.m.*

Mysterious afternoon.

Pascale emerged, the only sign of colour on her pallid form a large red love bite on her neck, as I was writing my last entry. She and Didier had an argument in which I heard my name. I expect she was defending me for getting drunk. The phone went a few times – involving long intense conversations – and then she dragged me out of the house. I asked her where she was taking me but she didn't say. We walked quite a long way, at one point through an underpass with traffic thundering over us, to a house a bit like hers, only smaller. A woman a bit younger than Mother, in black leggings and a large shirt, answered the door. She and Pascale talked while she looked me up and down. I felt uncomfortable and smiled like an idiot.

Then we went inside into the kitchen. At the table, a blonde girl with very red eyes sat in a towelling dressing gown. She gave a start when she saw me and began crying. No one paid much attention, though her mother said something that made her look at me and they all laughed.

We didn't stay long. On the way back, I asked her in French why her friend had been crying.

'Oh, just because. She is sad.'

'But why?'

'Because last night her boyfriend went to a party and got off with somebody else.' (I think I'm translating this correctly.)

'And why did she laugh at me?'

'Because you were the one her boyfriend got off with.'

Honestly! It seems she'd taken me there to make her friend feel better. 'Look at the frumpy English girl who seduced your boyfriend! Nothing to worry about there – he must have been drunk!'

It's so disorienting living in a foreign country. My French seems to be coming back to me; I'm not managing too badly, but it's still as if everyone is in on some private joke that I don't understand. You have to work so hard to keep up. And try and look deeply fascinated and fascinating while inside you feel quite stupid.

So, I arrived back here, feeling cross and bothered, and that's made me feel homesick. I wish – I've got to stop this – that I could talk to William. He never makes me feel foolish, or frumpy. I know he thinks my clothes are weird and he must like girls in make-up or he wouldn't be going out with Delilah – but when I'm with him, I feel interesting. Take that time the other day when we were cycling to school together and passed those trendy sixth-form girls in miniskirts and flowery wellies. William said, 'You're ahead of your time, Con, ahead of your time. You'll have to stop wearing wellies now, if they've actually become cool.' He sounded quite proud. I could have hugged him.

❤ Living (though atmosphere more 'dead') room, 4.30 p.m.

I was writing the above when the phone rang and Madame Blanc tiptoed up and tapped on the door.

I leapt to my feet and charged downstairs, my heart in my mouth, thinking 'My grandparents, les de Bellechasses!'

I had to take a deep breath before picking up the receiver. My hand was shaking. 'Hello,' I said. '*Bonjour.*'

'Con! It's me!'

'Delilah?'

'Guess where I am!'

'Er. At home?'

'No.'

'At William's house?'

'No.'

'Buckingham Palace?'

'No, stupid.'

'Dubai?'

'Con. That's not till half-term.'

'Skiing?'

'You know I've just been. Give up?'

'Yes.'

'PARIS!'

A variety of emotions fought their way across my heart at this point. Delilah is the only child of affluent parents. There is not much Delilah wants that Delilah doesn't get. It's just typical that if there's one thing I've got that she hasn't – in this case a French exchange trip to Paris – she should end up getting one too. At the back of my mind, I sometimes think she's only interested in William because he is – was – mine.

She started filling me in – her father had this friend from work, he'd relocated to the Paris office, had a daughter of our age, they lived on the Île de la Cité, yacht in the south of France, blah, blah – and suddenly I stopped feeling cross and all I could feel was relief: my friend Delilah was on the other end of the phone. My friend Delilah was in Paris!

I couldn't tell her everything that had happened to me because Didier was in the room, rustling a newspaper called L'Équipe. But I've checked it's OK with Madame Blanc and we have arranged to meet outside the Pompidou Centre tomorrow afternoon.

💜 *Still living (I am anyway) room, 5 p.m.*

Another phone call! Julie!

'Con,' she hissed. 'I've got to get away. I'm living in a house full of small children – including my French exchange, who's about ten. I'm going mad. Chatter,

chatter. Cartoons. Plastic toys everywhere. And I think they're poisoning me.'

'Poisoning you?'

'It's really weird. They put food on my plate and then they all sit back in their chairs and watch me while I eat it. And it tastes funny.'

'Are you sure they just don't want to see your appreciation of what they've made? The local delicacies, etcetera?'

'It's chicken nuggets, Con. And they taste different. They're poisoning me. When can I see you?'

I told her about Delilah and meeting her tomorrow outside the Pompidou Centre. She huffed about D (they've never liked each other, which can make things awkward) but she's going to join us anyway.

❤ *Encore living room, 7 p.m.*

Another phone call! Just call me Mademoiselle Popular.

'Hello?'

'Hello, Constance. *C'est François.*'

'François!'

I made a frantic face at the room. Pascale and her parents were watching television – a dubbed version of *Only Fools and Horses* which had been making me feel homesick. Only Didier seemed to notice, but he stared at me as if I was quite mad and then looked back down at his book.

'Please can we have a date?'

François – bless – had obviously been practising his English.

I said, 'François, I've met your girlfriend. She was crying. Or she was – until she saw me.'

'Pardon?'

'No, we can't have a date. Sorry. *Bonsoir.*' I hung up.

Didier, the patronizing creep, was laughing. Where does he get off?

💜 *Back in P's bedroom, 9 p.m.*

Three phone calls, but none from my grandparents. Why haven't they rung?

Chapter Five

New vocab: un *appartement très class* (a cool flat)

Monday 31 March

💜 *RER, line A, just past Nation, on the way home, 6 p.m.*

Very busy day, first chance to write in here.

This morning I went to Pascale's school. It was all a bit of a blur. It was their last day before the Easter holidays so there weren't proper lessons. All the children kissed each other on both cheeks when they met up. French teenagers *en masse* are much cleaner and tidier than English ones. You see a lot of outdoor wear – jackets saying 'Umbro' – but they aren't worn ironically, or fashionably, like they are at Woodvale Secondary, but more for practical reasons. I spent lessons not understanding a word and trying to look invisible at the back of the class and my free time trying to hide from François, who waved at me across the outdoor concourse. He'd have caught up with me if I hadn't ducked into the loo. There was no one from Woodvale there. They're all at different schools.

I was hoping Pascale wouldn't come to Paris. I told her Virginie, Julie's FE, wasn't coming, but she said she was coming too and nothing would shift her. I felt quite cross at first. Didn't she have an Eric to sneak away and snog or something?

We walked to the Pompidou Centre from the station at Châtelet-Les Halles. It's less grand there than in Saint-Germain-des-Prés: cheaper shops, more tourists, the odd homeless man with a dog on a string. I bought Marie some coloured glass beads and William a T-shirt with 'Vespa' on the sleeves because he's always said he wanted one (a Vespa, I mean, not a T-shirt). I hid it deep in my bag so Delilah wouldn't see it.

Delilah and Julie and another girl were already there, sitting on the ground, on a long, shallow step, in the shadow of the Pompidou. The outside of the building is extraordinary: blue and red and bubbly, like the dissection of a body or something Cyril might make with leftover Harry Potter Lego. I was so glad to see them I ran, leaving Pascale to catch up.

They jumped to their feet when they saw me and we all hugged. Then Delilah introduced me to Mimi, her French exchange girl. 'Hillo,' she said poshly and I remembered that she was English. She was wearing white linen trousers (which must have had a grey bum now from her sitting on the ground) and a light blue cardigan that crossed over and tied up at the back. Pale blonde bobbed hair. Très sophisticated. Then Pascale came up and I introduced her to the others. She smiled nervously. I had this uncharitable feeling of having the upper hand and for an awful, fleeting moment thought of somehow taking my revenge for the Crying Girl, but luckily managed to fight it down.

We had a hot chocolate and a crêpe at one of the cafes close by. Mimi, who gave the impression of knowing more than everyone else about everything, said it was 'rather overpriced', but I loved the fact that everyone was sitting staring out at the street in rows, as if they were at the cinema. Julie, Delilah and I ran through what we'd been up to; Pascale glowered, not really joining in; Mimi kept on translating the menu to us — even though we'd already ordered — just to show she could. (An English person speaking with a proper French accent actually sounds pretentious. This is an observation I should probably take to heart.) Julie and Delilah seemed to get on for once. Julie said Virginie, her FE, was wet and that she was really homesick. I couldn't say I was too because of Pascale being there. Delilah and I tried to convince Julie that she wasn't being poisoned, that she only thought that because she was feeling displaced. She said, 'Yeah, but you didn't have to eat last night's burger. It was, like, raw. And no bun.'

Mimi said, 'Steak tartare,' but we ignored her.

'Why would they want to poison you? What's in it for them?' I said.

Nobody could think of an answer to that.

We walked round the shops a bit more then – Delilah bought some eyeshadow, Julie a bright-pink scarf, Pascale a few beaded necklaces. Mimi wanted to go to Gap. The others went in but I stood outside. I told them I wasn't wasting a minute of my time in Paris in some American capitalist conglomerate. 'Stay there then and smell the car fumes,' said Julie. When they came out, loaded with bags, we walked down some more small streets, across a busy road, past a really posh hotel called Hôtel de Ville, and down to the Seine. I made everyone stop so I could breathe in the smell – brown and dank and delicious. Then we crossed a bridge, which was covered in scaffolding, to an island called Île de la Cité. And here, in a little street, was Mimi's apartment.

It was *amazing*. It was everything I –

Here's our stop. More later.

♥ P's *bedroom, 7 p.m.*

I'll have to describe it in detail.

1. Entry through tall double doors into a little courtyard with a fountain in the middle. Moroccan-style tiled floor. Door over to left to . . .
2. The most wonderful creaky, cranky cage-like lift,

with brass knobs and a double door like an elegant gate which took you to . . .

3. Third-floor apartment – with view of glamorous white roofs and snaking river from the living room. Also . . .

4. Wooden floors, two white sofas, marble fireplace and . . .

5. Three bedrooms including Mimi's – stylishly minimalist, one canopy bed, one mattress on the floor. (Something I have that Delilah hasn't – a bed!)

Mimi's parents, who, according to Delilah, are really really (or rather 'rilly, rilly') nice, were out, so we just lazed around in the sitting room, eating several bars of chocolate we found in the fridge. (French chocolate bars have nothing on Cadbury's.) Pascale spent a long time in the loo and Mimi had a long, giggly phone call with a friend, so I made the most of the time to tell J and D about François and his insistent tongue, which made them both laugh a lot.

Julie said, 'I'm not getting off with anyone while I'm here because my heart belongs to Karl.'

'Me too,' Delilah said.

We all thought that was hilariously funny and fell about laughing.

'Not Karl, William,' she squealed, finally. 'My heart belongs to William. I'm going to be faithful to William.'

I felt a pang so, to suppress it, I said, 'Ah well, not me.

I'm free and single. Watch out the Parisian male. Unless your name's François.' And that set us all off laughing again.

We had such a nice time. No grown-ups, no school, no parents, no home at all. It was like the essence of friendship. It was horrible when we had to leave.

Mimi mentioned that we weren't far from Saint-Germain-des-Prés so I persuaded Julie and Pascale to do a quick detour past my grandparents' apartment and get the metro back to the RER from there. All three of us were tired so we walked in silence across another bridge and down Boulevard Saint-Germain. When we got to the building, there was a different concierge on the door. There were lights on the upper floors. A woman was standing by one of the windows; a small boy stared out of another.

'So, are you going to see if they're in?' asked Julie.

'No.'

'Why not?'

'Because of the letter. They'll contact me if they want to . . .'

I stood staring up. Julie lit a cigarette. Pascale bummed one off her, but I could tell she didn't normally smoke by the way it kept going out.

'OK. Let's go,' I said. We turned and started walking down the street, back in the direction of the river. Halfway down, an elderly couple came towards us. The man, thinning grey hair, stooped shoulders, wearing a thick green coat and what you would have to describe as a handbag over his shoulder, was talking intently. The woman, much smaller, with a grey bob and a pretty lined face, appeared to be listening, but she was also looking into the window of the shop we were passing, where the mannequin was wearing a slate-blue wool suit.

I didn't say anything, but I *knew*. When we got to the end of the street, I turned and I was right. They were walking into the apartment block. I knew as surely as if it had been written across their foreheads that they were my grandparents.

I haven't said anything to the others. They won't understand why I didn't just introduce myself, why I didn't just walk up and say hello.

I'm not sure myself. I keep thinking they don't want to meet me. Otherwise, why wouldn't they ring?

❤ *P's bedroom, 8 p.m.*

Two phone calls from François. Both times I've pretended to be out.

And one phone call from Delilah. Several items from Mimi's bedroom have gone missing.

1. A diamanté evening bag.
2. A pair of silver earrings in the shape of dolphins.
3. A tube of Lancôme cherry lipgloss.

Did either of us 'accidentally' pick any of it up?

I said, 'No, no, Mimi must have mislaid them,' but MORTIFICATION. I'm going to have it out with Pascale RIGHT NOW.

💜 *P's bedroom, 8.10 p.m.*

Flat denial from my thieving French exchange. She even emptied out her bag to show me how empty it was. I'll have to wait until she's asleep and *go through her stuff.*

💜 *Under P's bed, 11 p.m.*

Item: One diamanté evening bag.
Item: A pair of silver earrings in the shape of dolphins.
Item: A tube of Lancôme cherry lipgloss.
Item: One unwashed white sports sock. (Actually cancel that – it was probably there already.)

Chapter Six

New vocab: *faire partie de* (to belong); *les biens personnels* (personal belongings)

Tuesday 1 April
♥ *Bathroom, 8 a.m.*

Woke up v. v. v. early feeling sick about the stash under Pascale's bed, and miserable about the fact that my grandparents haven't got in contact. I cheered up when I got downstairs to find a postcard of a red bus from Mother and a fax from William waiting for me on the breakfast table.

Mother's postcard, posted the day I left, says:

Chérie – hope all is well and you are having lovely, lovely, lovely time. We miss you, but are

busy decorating your room for your return.
À bientôt, Maman.

Then there are some xxxs (kisses) and oooos (hugs) – in pink felt-tip, which must have been added by Marie.

William's fax, sent to the Blancs' fax machine from the newsagent's at the end of our road, begins, 'Oi, you,' which doesn't bode well. (He can be so uncouth. I can't imagine Delilah putting up with that sort of talk for a minute.) It lists all the things he's been doing: helping his brother clear out the shed; visiting his grandmother in her home in Epsom; watching Liverpool v. AC Milan on the big-screen TV at the local pub . . . 'until my dad came in'. (Most people's fathers might have kicked them out if they found them in the local pub. William's would have been too drunk to notice. Poor William, I bet, will have slipped away embarrassed.)

At the end, he's written, 'Wonder if they sell chocolate buttons in Paris.' (He and I have a thing about chocolate buttons.) 'Wonder if they taste the same without me! Love, William.'

It's not what you'd call a love letter. Or even a love fax. But I've spent half an hour studying the last sentence. What does he mean, do they taste the same without him? Is he saying the ones he's had don't taste the same without me? Is it a way of saying I make a difference to his life, or at least to his enjoyment of chocolate buttons? What does the exclamation mark mean? Am I overanalysing? Should I now shut up?

❤ Dining table, 9 a.m.

Didier, who keeps giving me the sort of look you might give a guinea pig that needs cleaning out, has just suggested they take me to visit Fontainebleau, which is a château not far away. I said that would be lovely but maybe this afternoon (this morning I've got secret plans). Madame Blanc glanced up from the oven, which she was in the middle of cleaning, and said that would suit her better too. Gives her a chance to sort out the house, she said. Poor woman.

I'm going to go into town before Pascale gets up.

❤ Starbucks, Les Halles, 10 a.m.

Just realized I've wasted twenty minutes of my time in Paris in an American capitalist conglomerate. Oh well, a Mango Frappuccino's a Mango Frappuccino.

I'm waiting for Delilah. I rang her from a phone box at the RER to tell her I had 'the goods'. She's agreed to meet me here and smuggle them back into Mimi's bedroom.

I've just struggled through another chapter of *Madame Bovary*. I don't know whether you're supposed to like her or hate her. She is married to an oaf, and she can be forgiven for looking for love elsewhere, but anyone who refers to 'bells of evening' or 'voices of nature' tends to lose my vote.

Oh, here's Delilah.

Mission accomplished. 'You can't bring Pascale to the apartment again,' said Delilah, who has been a sport. 'I'm not going to keep on being your trafficker. They're going to start suspecting me. It's not on.'

'No, I know it's not. Just this time. You're a star.'

I handed her the stuff wrapped in a plastic bag. She had to get back – Mimi and her parents were taking her for lunch somewhere posh called Les Deux Magots (The Two Maggots? Surely not – I must have misheard), but I managed to ask her idly if she'd had any letters from home yet and she said, 'No.'

'I've only been here a couple of days,' she added shortly.

'Of course,' I said. But deep down, all I could think was, 'Hurray! William has faxed me! Hurray!'

Isn't that awful? I've got to stop it, I really have. Delilah is my friend. I had my chance with William and I blew it. I promise I won't do it again.

(Oh God, sorry. Just one more little one ... hurray!)

❤ *Dining table, 1 p.m.*

Pascale met me, boot-faced, when I got back from Paris. She has obviously discovered what I have done – or undone. On the RER I rehearsed a lecture on Why Stealing Is Wrong, but I've decided not to give it. It's her business. Just so long as she keeps out of mine.

The Crying Girl is here for lunch. I'm going to make myself scarce.

♥ *P's bedroom, 6 p.m.*

Back from Fontainebleau. Alive. Just.

After lunch, Didier, who passed his test two weeks ago, drove Pascale and me to Fontainebleau. Madame Blanc said she couldn't come because she had a headache, and took herself up to bed. There is something mysterious about that woman. The others had got into the car (a beaten-up three-door Citroën) but I came back upstairs because I'd forgotten my purse and the door to her bedroom was wide open and she wasn't in it. She wasn't in the bathroom either. She must have gone out.

The journey was hairy. Didier kept swerving into the middle of the road. Pascale and I screeched half in horror, half in delight, every time he turned a corner.

We didn't bother with the château – too pricey. Instead, we bought a box of gâteaux from a shop and sat on our coats and ate the cakes in the gardens. The sun came out and it was so warm I took off my jumper. I was wearing an old green T-shirt that seems to have shrunk recently and I felt self-conscious. I saw Didier look at me – then he leant across and tickled the inside of my elbow with a blade of grass. I laughed and it was OK.

I don't get Didier. Sometimes he looks down his nose like he's about fifteen years older than me; other times he's almost playful. I feel him staring and I don't know whether he's about to say something, or whether he's checking I'm all right. Today I quite liked him. Or I did until he mentioned François.

'Have you seen your little friend again?' he said. Little friend! I mean, that's *so* condescending.

'No. Been too busy.' I decided not to be drawn.

'I hear he is quite smitten with the English girl.'

'I don't know about that,' I said.

'What are you talking about?' asked Pascale, because we'd been talking in English.

'Ahh,' Didier replied, ignoring her. 'So, he is in love. And this William, he misses you?'

I glared at him. 'Have you been reading my private faxes?'

He put his hands up as if in surrender. 'I am but the delivery boy.'

The way he went on, anyone would think I was some femme fatale, instead of the only girl in Woodvale who's never had a boyfriend.

He drove v. fast all the way home. If he weren't so grown-up, you'd think he was showing off.

♥ Living room, 7 p.m.

Two phone calls to report.

I rang Delilah to check everything was OK. She said it was fine. She'd put each item back and thinks suspicion has already lifted. A few minutes ago, Mimi had found the necklace and said, 'Oh, it was here all the time!'

I was about to hang up when she said, 'Oh, and Con, guess what? William just rang me! I felt a bit worried earlier when you asked if I'd heard from him so I sent him a text. He rang me straight back and everything's fine. He's so great. I mean, you know that, don't you, he's your friend. But I think I love him, you know? I think he's The One. Before I started going out with him, I was all over the place. But now I feel grounded. Do you know what I mean?'

I said I did.

If there was anything sad in my voice she didn't notice. 'And he's such a great kisser!' she added.

I rang Julie to cheer myself up. She sounded a bit better – Virginie's got a secret wild side, apparently, but said she thinks she's just eaten horse.

♥ My bed, 10 p.m.

A conversation with Pascale has made me like her again. During supper Monsieur Blanc kept getting at her.

He bellowed, in English, 'So, I hope you are fluent now, Pascale, as you have Constance here to remind you of your tenses. I hope you are making the most of this opportunity to increase your vocabulary,' etc., etc. Everyone was nervous. Madame Blanc was scratching at a mark on the table, while Didier made overly appreciative noises about the food.

Pascale stared at her father insolently and then pushed her plate away and stood up.

'Sit down,' he said.

'No,' she said. And then there was a big row. I cleared the table quickly and then came up here to write to William. I was telling him everything – about Madame Blanc's cleaning and Didier's driving and Pascale's nicking – when Pascale stormed into the room, red-faced, swore a few times, sat on her bed and burst into tears. I went over and put my arm round her shoulders.

'He hates me,' she said, rubbing mascara into her cheeks. 'I do everything wrong. He only likes my brother Philippe. Nothing any of the rest of us do is right.'

'No, no,' I said soothingly.

'It's true. He thinks I am a delinquent.'

It wasn't the time to raise the shoplifting and the thieving. 'I'm sure he doesn't,' I said. 'Parents are hard.'

I tried to make her laugh by telling her all about Mother and some recent attempts of mine to matchmake her. 'Of course she ended up with someone I'd never have chosen, our "geeky" landlord, Mr Spence.'

'Geeky?' she said. 'What does "geeky" mean?'

'Odd, unusual, a bit weird.'

She looked at me hard. 'Like you?' she said.

And I must have been in a good mood because we both laughed.

Later on, I told her about William: about how much I liked him and how much Delilah, his girlfriend, liked him too. Pascale said, 'You need to forget him. You need to meet someone else. You can't lose a friend. You can't lose two friends.'

I nodded. When she was asleep I tore up the letter to William. I've got to stop thinking about him. I'm in Paris. It should be easy.

Pascale's all right really, she is.

Chapter Seven

New vocab: un *collier en argent* (a silver necklace); *les lunettes de soleil* (sunglasses); un *tampon* (a tampon)

Wednesday 2 April
💜 *P's bedroom, 6 p.m.*

I couldn't sleep last night, thinking about my grandparents. I was joking to Julie the other day about how they were my *entrée* into French society, but it's not about that. It's not that I don't love my half-siblings or Jack, my ex-stepfather, or Granny Enid, his mother, my step-grandmother. Because I do. I really do. I suppose I just wanted to meet a bit of family that was *mine*. My father was an orphan, so there's nothing on that side – except for some uncle or other in New Zealand. I just realized I wanted to look into someone's face and see something I recognized. And maybe to feel connected. Not just for my sake, either. Mother puts a brave face on everything and I know she thinks of London as her home, but she can look a little lost sometimes – at school sessions or meeting parents of my friends. It must be good to be comfortable with your place in a family, to have somewhere where you always feel at home.

I woke up, determined to sort it out. If they don't want anything to do with me or Mother, fine. But I had to know.

Pascale had told me she planned to sneak out to see Eric today. He works in a garage that fits exhaust pipes and Wednesday's his day off. Perfect, I thought. But then first thing this morning he rang to say he needed to get his Suzuki's gasket mended so she decided to come with me instead.

The house was empty when we got up. Monsieur Blanc had gone off to work early; Madame Blanc was out – probably at the *supermarché*. Didier was doing some schoolwork at the dining-room table. He was wearing a black T-shirt that had seen more than its fair share of washes and a pair of grey slacks even I know aren't the height of fashion.

'Do you have plans today?' he said when he saw us putting our jackets on.

'Eiffel Tower,' I said quickly.

'Ah.' He stretched his arms into two 'V's behind his head and then out straight. 'Maybe I'll come.'

Pascale stopped in the doorway. She blew out through her teeth and jabbered something I didn't get. He shrugged and turned back to his work. 'OK.'

She rolled her eyes behind his back and did the blowing out thing again (I wish I could describe it exactly – it was so fantastically French).

On the way to the RER she said Didier was an imbecile, but that Philippe – who'll be back at the weekend – is fantastic. She nodded to herself. 'Him,' she said, 'you will love.' I am getting a bit bored of hearing about the wonders of Philippe (particularly as Monsieur Blanc seems to think he's so great) but Pascale got a photograph out of her wallet and . . . well, he *is* handsome. If you like big eyebrows, anyway.

We got the metro, as before, to Saint-Germain-des-Prés. I'd been full of determination when we left the house but as we got close to the apartment block I felt it drain away. When I breathed out it was as if I was going to deflate and deflate and deflate. My internal cavities seemed to fuse together. I could hardly put one step in front of the other without falling over. What if they just closed the door in my face? What if they'd read my letter and found it rude and had decided they didn't want to know me? What if . . .

We stood outside the door – me feeling sick, Pascale whistling, so clearly not feeling sick.

'I can't do it,' I said.

There was a cafe opposite I hadn't noticed before. I pulled her towards it and sat down at a table in the second row facing the street. And that was when I realized something important. This was what I'd come for.

I don't mean the cafe, with its little round French tables, its French wicker chairs, its French fan whirring, its French waiter with his big, wide, white French apron coming over with his big, wide, white French menu. None of this mattered. I could have been anywhere. I could have been in Bombay. Or Bolton. It wasn't Paris I'd come to find, was it? I'd come to find my grandparents. I suppose I've known this all along, but it came as a shock.

'OK. I'm going to do it,' I said before the waiter could reach us. But at that minute, the elderly woman I'd seen the other day, the one with the neat grey bob, the one I was convinced was my grandmother, came out of her apartment block opposite. I didn't stop to think. I pushed back my chair, jumped up and ran out of the cafe.

I stopped on the pavement. The woman had turned towards Boulevard Saint-Germain and was walking smartly and purposefully down the street away from me.

'What are you doing?' Pascale had come out too.

'Sssh,' I said. 'That's her. Let's go.'

We followed about ten metres behind her. She was wearing a maroon skirt with a pine-green jacket, and a patterned scarf in the same colours round her neck. She walked quickly, but occasionally she stopped to look in a shop window. She crossed Boulevard Saint-Germain and turned into a side street. We passed a toyshop and then a shop selling baby knits, and for a moment I allowed myself to think how my life might have been if my mother hadn't run away from home, how Sundays might have been spent with my grandparents, ambling round these streets – a little light shopping, a play in the park, *steak frites* for lunch . . .

My grandmother had sped up and Pascale was beginning to dawdle, so I had to pull her along. We reached the river and crossed a bridge – a different one from the one we crossed the other day – and not far away on the other side was a department store called La Liberté. We tried to look inconspicuous as we followed my grandmother into the store.

We were in a large cosmetics hall. It felt airy and empty because there was no ceiling in the middle – just blue railings going up and up to floor after floor, like an enormous staircase.

My grandmother looked at some Lancôme face creams, dabbing them on her hand and smelling them. She took the escalator to the first floor, where she tried on a black polo-neck jumper. She then took the lift to the fifth floor, where she went into 'les toilettes' (we hovered at a discreet distance). On the way out, she browsed in the books section before returning, via the escalators, to the ground floor. I began to worry we might be rather obvious, and wished Pascale wasn't with me – that goth black is so in your face.

'Why don't you talk to her?' she hissed. We were in the accessories section on the ground floor. My grandmother was the other side of a display case, holding up a watch with a silver strap, peering at the face as if she couldn't quite make out the numbers.

'Because it's not the right moment,' I hissed in return.

I wouldn't have known what the right moment looked like if I'd had it laid out in front of me. Golden? Maybe silver. Or white perhaps? But the air around it would have been calm and generous and warm. It may be that the right moment never existed. Or maybe I had left it behind in Boulevard Saint-Germain. It's funny what a difference a few seconds can make. If I'd gone straight up to the apartment block and not gone into the cafe. If my grandmother had come out of the building earlier. If I'd run fast up behind her and introduced myself before she'd crossed the road. If Eric hadn't needed a new gasket. If Didier had come too. If a butterfly hadn't beaten its wings a hundred years ago in Costa Rica . . . Any of these things might have prevented what happened next.

'What does that mean, "the right moment"?' Pascale was up close to me when she said this – I'm sure of it, looking back. That was the right moment, or anyway the moment as far as she was concerned. She was looking around nervously. I can't quite remember, but I think she put her arm around me and that she peered into my face. I took this as concern. Misdirection more like.

My grandmother was putting the silver watch back and was asking to look at another. I had my eyes on her so I didn't see the man come up behind me. 'The right moment?' I began. 'It's —'

'*Excusez moi, mademoiselle.*' A security guard had put his hand on my shoulder. A woman, hair the colour of dead grass, with a name badge on her jacket, was standing next to him. Her chin jutted in my direction. She said something which must have meant 'empty your pockets' but I hadn't worked out what was happening, or what she was saying, so I just stared at her. So, then the security guard said something to her and she began frisking me. I was wearing that jacket from Oxfam — grubby green suede — that I'm pretty fond of. The only thing is the pocket linings have frayed away and anything put in them tends to fall into the hem at the bottom. I know that — I've lost a couple of ten-pence pieces down there and the odd bit of tissue — nothing else. But Pascale didn't know that.

'Pascale!' I cried. She was edging away, the little cow! She was way over towards the gloves and handbags. 'Come back!' I yelled. Until now, it had been very discreet, no one had raised their voice. But at this, lots of people looked round at us, including — oh God, no . . . yes — my grandmother.

The woman in the suit had found what she was looking for. The security guard made me take the coat off and he rummaged around, his arm disappearing inside the lining like a vet's when delivering a calf. Then he passed something to the woman.

'Hah!' she said, holding up a silver necklace.

He passed something else.

'Hah!' she said again, holding up a pair of sunglasses.

He passed something else.

'Ehr?' she said.

Mortification: it was a battered tampon.

'I'm English,' I said. 'I'm sorry. It wasn't me. Believe me, please! PASCALE!'

I'm surprised Pascale hadn't scarpered. I suppose she thought that would look more guilty than staying. Maybe she hadn't thought it through. Maybe she was torn. Anyway, to give her her due, she came back.

She stood there sulkily.

'Pascale. Did you do this? Please tell them if you did. Tell them it wasn't me.'

I know my French isn't great, and I was so desperate my tenses were probably wrong, but she said, 'I don't understand you,' and looked away.

The security guard had got out his radio and was talking into it. He was keeping hold of me with his other hand.

'Can I help, please?'

The woman with the neat grey hair – my grandmother – had come across. She spoke in English. I looked into her face – I had no doubt now: it was lined and papery, but her eyes were the same shape, the same nut-brown, as Mother's – and my own eyes welled with tears. This was awful. It was not how it was meant to be. I opened my mouth but no words came out. I didn't know what to say. I'm Constance? Why haven't you rung me? Or should I pretend to be someone else? Was this it? Would I never be able to tell her who I was? Was this the first and last time we would ever meet? Was I about to be thrown into prison for the rest of my life?

'I . . .' I began to speak but it turned into a wail. 'Pascale! Please . . .'

Two policemen with guns arrived on the shop floor and were walking towards us. Pascale's eyes filled with panic and she turned and ran. It was the best thing she could have done – for me anyway – because the security guard shouted and one of the policemen ran after her and caught her by the changing rooms. She struggled in his arms, but he dragged her over towards us.

My grandmother had been talking to the woman in the suit and now she turned to me and said, 'I speak English. I will come to translate for you.'

It was all too, too dreadful. I thought if I didn't answer she might go away, but she didn't. The security guard, the woman in the suit, the two policemen – and their guns – and my grandmother led Pascale and me to the lifts and to an office behind the children's clothes on the second floor. We were made to sit on chairs by the wall. They obviously thought we were a teenage gang: the Connie and Clyde of the shoplifting fraternity. I kept shaking my head and saying, 'I didn't do it. I didn't do it,' but they just ignored me.

The security guard left, leaving the policemen at the door, and the woman got out a form, which she placed next to the necklace and the sunglasses and — please! — the battered tampon in front of her. She jerked her chin at us and said something.

'They need your names,' said my grandmother. 'And then you will go with the police.'

I looked at her dumbly.

Pascale said, 'Sophie Danone.'

They just looked at her.

Grumpy, but resigned, she said, 'Pascale Blanc.'

There was a silence. The woman in the suit looked up at me. Everyone was waiting.

So, this was it. This would have to be the right moment.

I stared into my grandmother's face.

'Connie Pickles,' I said.

Chapter Eight

New vocab: *on a fait savoir la famille* (the relatives have been informed)

Same day
💜 *Bathroom, 9 p.m.*

I didn't want to leave off there, but I had to go downstairs for supper. No sign of Pascale or her father, just Madame, Didier *et moi*. It was a sticky, silent meal. His father not being in the room, Didier switched the television off, so there wasn't even that to dilute the tension. I couldn't wait to leave the table.

It's a relief to be back in the privacy of my own diary.

My grandmother looked at me and put her hand to her mouth. Her voice trembled. 'Constance?'

'Yes,' I said. 'Oui.'

She didn't hug me then. She hugged me later, after she'd persuaded the higher echelons of La Liberté not to *presser les charges* (or whatever they do in France); after Pascale's parents had been telephoned; and after we'd been escorted from the premises, with a warning from them and a promise from us never to do it again. (I had to promise too, which was very enraging as I didn't do anything in the first place.) We landed on the street, and my grandmother stopped a taxi and bundled us both in. She sat in the front and it wasn't until we were on the pavement outside her apartment block that she put her arms round me and held me to her. She felt frail and brittle. I was like a giant against her. When she pulled apart she said, 'Constance. I would not have known. You are not like your mother. You must look like your father, no? Though now I look, your mouth . . . it is like Bernadette's. Yes, I see my Bernadette in your mouth.'

My mother is slim and very petite. It's quite galling actually. 'I'm a bit fatter than usual,' I said hopefully. 'It's all those French *pâtisseries*.'

We went through the doors then, past the concierge, who winked at me, and upstairs to the apartment where she took our jackets and made us sit in the drawing room while she rang Pascale's parents to tell them where we were and prepared coffee. It wasn't small, but the furniture felt like it had come from a bigger house. A large wardrobe – which she later told me was called a *buffet* – took up one side of the room. There was a formal dining table and chairs in one corner, and a big brown velvet sofa, where we sat, in the other. Paintings – lots of horses and hunting dogs and gloomy fruit bowls – covered the walls. Vases and china shepherdesses dotted every surface.

She came back in with cups and a plate of cakes on a tray. She moved some magazines from the mahogany coffee table, laid the tray down in front of us and sat in a leather armchair next to the sofa.

'So. My Constance,' she said. 'Ah.'

I told her I was glad she seemed so pleased to see me, that I'd been worried because she hadn't answered Mother's letter to say I was coming – she said she had never received it, so where did that go? – or phoned me, and she said, 'But how could I?' It turns out I'd written down one of the digits of the Blancs' phone number wrong. I am so STUPID.

She asked me all about Mother and she cried a little bit and said how sorry she was that Mother didn't speak to her, that she regretted her behaviour all those years ago but that my mother was so proud ... she broke off. 'It's all right,' I said. 'I don't mind what you say.'

'Well, he was not the man we wanted for Bernadette. He was not French, he was not Catholic, he had no job ...'

'He was an actor,' I said.

She looked at me.

'He was in that advert.'

'An advert?'

'It was for a drink called Cariibod. I think it was vodka and pineapple juice mixed. They don't make it any more. And . . .'

'And?'

'Well, that was it, I suppose. But you never know what might have happened.'

'If it hadn't been for his horrible, horrible motorbike accident. I know.'

Pascale was looking a bit left out, because all this went on in English, so then my grandmother asked her some questions about school, her parents and La Varenne. I noticed my grandmother sat back in the armchair when she talked to her, as if she might catch something like nits or herpes. It's the black make-up: it can be off-putting. Oh, and I suppose the shoplifting didn't help. I'm so relieved she seemed to believe I hadn't done it. Maybe she knew it in her bones. Our bones.

There was the sound of a key in the door and the stooped man in the heavy green coat walked into the room. He stopped short when he saw us girls huddled on the sofa and his face went white. His lips and cheeks and everything. It was as if the blood just drained away.

My grandmother jumped up and said, 'Pierre, this is Constance!'

He made a small movement towards Pascale and she stood up and put out her hand.

'Constance!' he said, and there was a lot of emotion in his voice. Horror mainly.

'I'm Constance,' I said, standing up quickly. He turned

towards me. When I put out my hand, he cupped it in both of his and looked deep into my face, and this time he didn't say anything at all.

And then a loud bell pealed, and pretty soon Didier was up in the apartment, looking grim-faced and angrier than . . . well, than a very angry, angry thing. I introduced him to my grandparents and he was courteous, but the full significance of the occasion may have been lost on him. He wanted us down into the car – and quick.

So, my grandparents kissed me goodbye, I left them with the correct phone number and promised to go for tea on Saturday.

In the car, Didier let rip. He put Pascale in the front of the Citroën and me in the back but there was none of the holiday atmosphere of yesterday's Fontainebleau trip. We drove back in heavy traffic and he talked at her the whole way. I felt sorry for her, particularly after she started crying – ugly, snotty sobs. Didier must have done too, because he calmed down, and when he got out of the car, he put his arm round her and left it there all the way to the house. I saw François out of the corner of my eye as I followed them. He was hanging around on the opposite side of the road. I bet he was waiting for me. I'd have felt freaked if I hadn't already felt freaked enough for one day.

Monsieur Blanc opened the front door and pulled Pascale into the kitchen. I came up to the bedroom and have only left for supper since. Raised voices – her shrieks, his low, heavy drone – still fill the house. I'm happy to have met my grandparents. I did feel a sort of connection, though maybe not the electric charge that I was hoping for. I don't know why, but I feel horribly homesick now. I wish I were anywhere other than here. I think back to how 'perfect' I thought this family sounded, how 'restful', and realize I couldn't have been more wrong. Just because a family looks nice on the outside doesn't mean it's nice on the inside. This one's full of wrong connections: it keeps fusing. It's as if all the people in it come from different families. I wish I was back in our small house in London, with Cyril and Marie running wild, and Mother regaling me with stories from the bra shop where she works and Jack, my stepfather, dropping in with his usual load of dodgy fish and knocked-off DVDs. It may be chaotic and unconventional, but it's home.

❤ *P's bedroom, 10 p.m.*

I still haven't seen the Eiffel Tower.

❤ *My bed, 11 p.m.*

(I miss William too.)

Chapter Nine

New vocab: *on est privé de sortir* (we're grounded)

Thursday 3 April
💗 *Bathroom,* 11 *a.m.*

We're grounded. Or rather, Pascale's grounded, so I might just as well be too.

Pascale is helping her mother vacuum and then scrub the tiles downstairs. I've been cleaning the bathroom. It was so pristine already it was about as useful an exercise as ironing an envelope. I found one pubic hair (yuck) behind the bidet, but otherwise it was spit-spot. It's a funny room, quite old-fashioned. There's this old white boiler above the bath and you have to put the hot tap on the right way to make it fire up.

I'm perched on the *toilette* now. I don't want to go

downstairs quite yet so I'm going to use the time for some self-examination.

I have been in France for almost a week.

Things achieved so far:

1. Cultural expansion of mind: I have seen the Pompidou Centre, Fontainebleau, a local market, several rooftop views of Paris as a whole.
2. Forging of new family ties: I have engineered a reunion with my grandparents.
3. Moral instruction of exchange student: I may have been partly instrumental in teaching Pascale The Wrongs of Shoplifting (and Theft in General).
4. Snog (third), not unsuccessful: 7.5/10

Things still to be achieved:

1. Eiffel Tower: you can't come to Paris and not see the Eiffel Tower.
2. Reunite Mother with my grandparents/her parents.
3. Spend remaining euros: buy something black?
4. Forget William.

The most important is number two. I've got to get Mother to Paris. I was longing to ring her last night, but I didn't dare ask to use the phone, the atmosphere being what it was. I'm going to ring her in a minute and come straight out with it. She needs to get on a train and come to Paris herself. It's the only thing for it. In fact, I'm going to ask if I can use the phone right NOW.

❤ *Bathroom again, 11.10 a.m.*

That was stupid of me. She was at work. Jack answered. He'd come round to look after Cyril and Marie (his mother, Granny Enid, usually helps out but she's at St George's this week getting a new hip).

I asked him how the fish were going – his latest scheme has been selling them door to door – but apparently the floor's fallen out of the door-to-door fish market. 'Cut-glass fruit bowls, Con,' he said. 'That's where it's at now.'

'What do you mean?' I said. 'Mail order?'

'Yeah. Nah. That sort of thing. Offices, Con. Deliveries. People don't like to buy different bits of fruit. They don't want to have to pick and choose themselves. They like it presented. Pretty bowl on the desk to pick at. Bit of banana. Bit of apple. A plum. Easy money, Con.'

'Don't tell me. You've "come into" some cut-glass fruit bowls and you're cooking up plans to offload them?'

'Raw fruit, Connie. I keep telling you.'

'Jack. I don't care if it's cooked or raw. You're stewed.'

'Connie, you're a cruel girl. Anyone ever tell you that?'

He is infuriating, but I do love him. I've left a message for Mother to ring me back. Urgently.

❤ *The very clean living room, 6 p.m.*

We've just been allowed out for a walk. Madame Blanc, who was putting on her mac and leaving the house herself, looked at our glum faces and relented. I suppose that means we're no longer technically grounded.

We went down to the square but the market wasn't on today. It was a car park instead. It was drizzling. All the houses seemed greyer today, and shrunken, as if they had hunched down into their coats. We went into a bar, empty except for a couple of boys playing pool, for a hot chocolate and Pascale ranted about how boring La Varenne was, how she wished she lived in the city, how suburban her parents were, how she was longing to escape. Sounded just like me and William in fact. She rang Eric, who was out. She talked some more about Philippe, who's coming home tomorrow. I told her I was looking forward to meeting him. She went quiet. She's got a sore on her lip that she keeps touching with her tongue.

I had an idea. I said we should ring Julie, which we did, and she said we could go over. She's only one stop on the RER and a short walk. It's funny, but I'd thought of her as miles away, back in London or the other side of the universe, unapproachable. But she's really quite close.

Madame Leboeuf, the mother of her French exchange, answered the door, and I have to say she's very nice for a poisoner. Dyed hair, jolly face, plump on top, skinny legs (one of those women who look like they might be pregnant but they can't be because they're too old). She seemed to know Pascale already and kissed her on both cheeks. Then she SCREAMED in my ear so loudly I almost crashed into the wall. I thought she'd gone mad but she was just shouting for Virginie and Julie, who came running down the stairs. Virginie and Pascale kissed on both cheeks, and Julie and I gave each other a hug. Then we went back upstairs to a sort of playroom/den where there were three children about the same ages as Cyril and Marie doing puzzles, and a big TV and a PlayStation, which were both on.

We didn't stay long. Julie seemed OK. She and Virginie are getting on fine. Secret dark side or no secret dark side, Virginie seemed a bit dull (ironic that Julie, who's always trying to lose her virginity, should be saddled with another one). Madame Leboeuf brought us a drink of something called grenadine – like fruit cordial, but gross – and a slice of cake that tasted of potpourri. When I bit into it Julie winced and shook her head at me. She might be right. It wasn't poison, but it was close.

Conversation was mainly general: half French, half English. I didn't have a chance to tell J anything about the shoplifting, the arrest, or the reunion with my grandparents. I began at one point. I said, 'So, yesterday, we went to Paris and –' But Julie interrupted. 'Did you?'

she said. 'Oh, so did we,' and then she went on about how she'd dropped in on Delilah and they'd gone to this cafe for lunch and what a great time they'd had . . . So, the two of them obviously don't hate each other any more. I'm very glad. That's a very good thing. I mean, it was always awkward before, and if they've bonded over a *croque-monsieur* without me, well, great. Fantastic in fact. Couldn't be better. I'm *thrilled*.

Chapter Ten

New vocab: *j'ai changé mon look* (I have had an image rethink)

Friday 4 April
❤ *P's bedroom, 5 p.m.*

Since lunch I have eaten:

1. Two hunks of baguette with butter and apricot jam.
2. One chocolate eclair (bit disappointing, it had custard inside not cream).
3. Three small heart-shaped biscuits called *palmiers*.
4. Two triangles of La Vache qui rit.

Can you tell I'm bored? Apparently, we're still grounded. Didier is around today – listening to classical music in his room – so Madame Blanc is pretending to be strict. When Pascale shrieked, 'But you let us out yesterday!' she looked panicked.

'Sssssh,' she said, her brown eyes hooded, and went back to her dusting. Philippe is coming back from his school trip tonight and she wants it to be extra clean. I've never met anyone so sad.

I thought Mother might ring me back yesterday evening, but she didn't.

I feel cross about Julie and Delilah becoming friends. There. I've said it. Does this mean I'm a horrible person? I always used to moan about what a pain it was that they didn't get on. I used to have to adjudicate between them as if they were rowing siblings. Julie thinks Delilah is posh and stuck-up, being at private school and all that. Delilah covers the fact that she's scared of Julie with a sort of breathy arrogance. But now they're all chummy and I feel left out. What does that say about me? Not a lot.

And I'm fed up with Madame Bovary. She's got a little girl called Berthe whom she ignores, and I know her husband is boorish, but why doesn't she just leave him? Mother had the nous to leave Jack – though that was different, because he kept having affairs.

And I'm fat. I've done nothing but eat cake since I got here. I've got two – no, three – ginormous spots the size of Versailles on my nose. They were smaller – more like Notre Dame – but I've just spent half an hour squeezing them. (Why is squeezing spots so satisfying? It's almost as satisfying as searching Marie's scalp for nits.) When you see me, they're the first thing you notice. Also I don't know what to do about my hair. It's long and straight like a nun's veil. (Only not black and white obviously, but mousy.) Pascale has just said I should I cut it. In fact she's just said *she* should cut it. Ha, ha. Naturally, I took one look at her punk-goth-black-spike-car-crash of a hairstyle and said, 'No way, baby, no way.'

I'm not *that* bored.

💜 *Bathroom, 5.30 p.m.*

Oh God.

💜 *P's bedroom, 5.35 p.m.*

We're not talking car crash. We're talking motorway pile-up, involving several jackknifed vans and an articulated lorry. Pascale says it'll be fine if I dye it mahogany. As if I'd let her dye it mahogany.

💜 *Bathroom, 5.40 p.m.*

Oh God, God, God.

❤️ *P's bedroom, 7.10 p.m.*

I can never go out – I can never leave this room
– again.

❤️ *P's bedroom, 7.12 p.m.*

Pascale looked out of the window, squealed and bounded
out of the room. I can hear loudly overlapping voices
and shrieks of laughter downstairs. There's a male voice
I don't recognize. Philippe must be home. Tough. I'm
staying here. I have no interest in meeting him. I know
I'm going to hate him.

❤️ *P's bedroom, midnight*

What can I say?

I've got butterflies in my stomach. My mouth is dry
like a stone. I keep fiddling with my mouth, twisting
my lips and biting them.

I realize why this house has been so quiet. It's because
when Philippe's not in it everything is suspended, like
a DVD on pause. Pascale has laughed all evening. Madame
Blanc took off her apron for the first time and even
Monsieur Blanc made jokes, tried to kiss his wife and
wrestled with his children. Philippe's a wind that blows
everyone's dark clouds away. Didier was quieter than
usual, but he's quiet anyway, so it doesn't count.

I had to go down eventually. Monsieur Blanc called up to me and then Pascale came running up the stairs and said I had to go down.

When I edged into the room, Madame Blanc gasped.

'What's that?' Didier said.

'My hair,' I replied.

Philippe stepped forwards. He took my hand, bent down and kissed it. '*Enchanté, mademoiselle.*'

He's tall, though not as tall as Didier, but taller than, say, William, who's a midget in comparison. He's got hair the colour of conkers, lizard-green eyes and a silver stud in one ear.

Monsieur Blanc said, 'Pascale! What is the meaning of this?'

She hid behind Philippe. 'I'm sorry,' she said. 'It was an accident.'

Philippe started laughing. 'What is it, *ma petite chatte?*' he asked, tickling her.

'It's my hair,' I said again.

He looked at me seriously. 'Yes,' he said. 'I can see. A certain resemblance to a purple chicken, no?'

'No,' I said.

But everyone was laughing and the crisis passed. (For Pascale, at least. I still had purple hair.)

Supper was thin slices of lamb with small oval green beans. Philippe regaled us with lots of stories about the Dordogne – the rivers, the caves, the force-fed geese. We were on cheese when he turned to Pascale and said, 'And what have you been up to here? No mischief, I hope.'

Madame Blanc scraped her chair back. It made a noise like someone clearing their throat.

Monsieur Blanc told Philippe about the shoplifting.

Philippe rolled his eyes at Pascale, but there was a grin waiting to happen at the corner of his mouth and she giggled. Didier said something curt at which Philippe sat up very straight and made a face like someone in trouble with a teacher. And again everyone laughed.

After supper, he said he was going down to the bar in the main street. Pascale, darting a look at her father, said she was grounded and couldn't go too. 'Oh, let her,' said Philippe. 'Papa, be kind, be nice, remember being young.' And Monsieur Blanc just shrugged, and said it was OK as long as Philippe promised to bring us home.

At the bar, there were loads of people he knew. I didn't feel left out like I did last Saturday before the party. Eric was there and he and Philippe had a game of pool. Pascale and I sat on the edge of a table, swinging our legs and drinking Coke (no more Pernod for me, thanks very much). When Philippe stretched out his arms to hit the ball, his T-shirt rode up so you could see the bars of muscle on his stomach. It gave me a feeling inside that I don't know quite how to describe, like warm sand slipping through your fingers, or a wind reaching through your sleeves to ruffle the hairs on your arm.

He knew *everyone*. I watched him moving around the room, having a joke with those girls by the door, play-punching that group of boys by the bar. When he came back to us, it felt like a privilege.

That was before he started teasing me. He can be SO RUDE. I was wearing my green coat and he put it on and paraded around, on tiptoe to pretend he was on high heels. He said I looked like a Belgian pop star. I said I thought he thought I looked like a purple chicken. He said, 'That also.' I looked like both – a purple Belgian chicken pop star. He put some money in the jukebox and made us all dance. He and Pascale did something called le roc, in which he swung her under his arms and over. 'Your turn,' he said to me. I couldn't do it, but it didn't stop him – he spun me round and round until I felt dizzy.

But then some older girls and boys arrived and he horsed around with them. When he came over to us, he said, 'I'm off, my children. See you tomorrow.'

Pascale made a face. 'You promised Papa to take us home,' she said.

He chucked her under the chin and in the end she just laughed.

He and the group he'd been talking to began leaving and suddenly the bar was quiet again. Pascale and I decided to go home. I'm glad we left when we did because I saw François and the Crying Girl crossing the street heading for the bar.

Pascale and I walked back. When we got home, Madame and Monsieur Blanc were in bed. Didier was the only one up, reading L'Immoraliste by Gide on the leather sofa in the living room. He was angry Philippe hadn't brought us home. Philippe had promised, he said. Honestly, as if we needed looking after.

Mother rang when I was out. Bother: too late to ring her back now.

Chapter Eleven

New vocab: mon petit chou (my little cabbage)

Saturday 5 April
♥ *Kitchen, 8 a.m.*

Everyone's still asleep, but I'm wide awake so I've come downstairs. One strange thing – the front door's unlocked and Madame Blanc's coat isn't here. She's probably gone to stock up on Cif.

I can see my reflection in the cooker hood. My hair looks much worse now it's mussed. One side is longer than the other. I look like a cat that's got caught in the rain. I'm seeing my grandparents this afternoon for tea – I can't go looking like this. They'll disown me before they've properly owned me. I've still got twenty-three euros. I've left the others a note and I'm going out to do something about my hair.

♥ Métamorphose, 9 a.m.

They say they can fit me in. They've sat me down in a corner to wait. I've flicked through some magazines and I've found a picture of a beautiful girl with v. short hair. 'Comme ça,' I said. Of course, it's the girl I want to look like – bugger the hair – but we'll see.

I must do something about my image. These magazines are full of girls looking elegant and poised. I'm just a mess. I used not to care, but I don't want to look like a purple Belgian chicken pop star for the rest of my life.

Here goes. They're ready for me now.

♥ Métamorphose, 9.30 a.m.

I'm in a chair right by the window, waiting for a tint to do its business, and who do you think just crossed the road and rang a bell on the door between Méphisto, the shoe shop, and the pharmacie? Madame Blanc. The door opened and she went in and it closed behind her. I can't think what she's doing up there. She had a bag saying 'HyperCasino', so she'd obviously bought some groceries. Maybe she goes shopping for some bed-bound old lady who lives there.

Poor Madame Blanc. She is the saddest woman I've ever met. She has NO life. It's all cleaning and tidying and cooking for her bully of a husband, or shopping for old ladies. I will never be like that when I'm grown-up. I'm going to have a job; no, not a job, a career; no, not a career, a *vocation* (not quite sure what yet), and will be answerable to no one. My husband will do my cleaning and cooking. I might shout at him if I come home from a busy day at the office doing my job, or rather my vocation, to find he's thrown away an important newspaper. But I won't because we'll love each other so much. I expect he'll be handsome and French and be called something like Philippe . . . Oh, stop it, Connie.

❤ *Métamorphose*, 10.15 a.m.

Something intriguing has just happened.

Madame Blanc has just exited from the same door. Not alone. And not with a poor old lady either. With a tall, grey-haired man, smoking a pipe. They stood on the pavement talking. Perhaps he's her doctor, I thought. Or her osteopath. I'm sure there's a simple explanation.

And then he held his pipe away from his mouth and kissed her.

I don't mean on the cheek, in a French I've-only-just-met-you-but-I'm-courteous sort of way. On the lips. Although . . . I don't know. French people *are* more demonstrative than us. Maybe it's how osteopaths – who do tend to be quite intimate with a person's body (their backs anyway) – say goodbye.

Got to go – time for rinse and cut. More reflections

on the extremely morally serious matter later.

💜 Métamorphose, 10.30 a.m.

Does Madame Blanc have a bad back? Or is Madame Blanc having an affair?

💜 Back at the house, 12 noon

Everyone looked stunned when I walked in. They were all in the kitchen or dining room drinking coffee, arguing in a low-level manner, when they saw me. I didn't notice Madame Blanc flinch when I told them where I'd been. She did look at me very carefully, but then they all were, getting me to turn round so they could see my hair from the back, oohing and aahing in a very satisfying manner.

Didier said I looked *gamine*, which I think means boyish. Philippe said, '*Très chic, mon petit chou.*' Apparently, *petit chou* means little cabbage – are we talking Brussels sprout here? Pascale looks almost put out by all the attention I'm getting.

I'm going upstairs to look at myself in the mirror (haven't dared yet) and then search my suitcase for something suitable to wear for tea with my grandparents.

Madame Blanc is re-ensconced at the kitchen sink. She is standing in the same way as usual. Her back doesn't look any straighter. She looks just as glum.

I had a quick look at the door opposite the hairdresser's.

There were several plaques with names on them. One of them said 'Dr R. B. Montaigne'. Could be a medical practitioner. Then again, could be someone with a doctorate in Medieval History.

Chapter Twelve

New vocab: *quelle taille?* (what size?); *grosse comme un éléphant* (as big as an elephant)

Same day
❤ P's *bedroom*, 6 p.m.

Meant to take this diary with me but forgot. Need to write quickly as Pascale, who is out, will be back any minute.

Lovely afternoon. Lovely, lovely afternoon.

Grand-mère – as she's asked me to call her – is the kindest person I've ever met. Grand-père is gruff but I think he's just shy. He's had a really hard life. His father was killed in the war and his mother died of cancer when he was a teenager. Bernadette – my mother – was his only child and I think it broke his heart when she ran off. Grand-mère says they shouldn't have been so angry with her – they realize that now – but that she had been so young and they were worried about her. They thought if they told her she was disinherited it would make her see sense. It didn't . . . but by then it was too late.

My grandfather stood up and left the room when she said this. 'He's a very proud man,' she continued. 'It was very hard for him. For both of us.'

We were a little bit awkward with each other. I didn't feel, as I'd hoped I might, that I'd known them for ever. I suppose life isn't like it is in books. I was trying so hard to be nice and grown-up so they'd like me. I was worried they might be disappointed. Grand-mère made a comment about Pascale early on – something like, was she really the sort of person I should be mixing with? I don't think she should have said that. She liked my haircut very much, but when she complimented me on it I felt her sort of look my Oxfam summer dress over as if she was mentally holding it up with tweezers. (It was the best thing in my suitcase.) Mother once told me her mother was a snob and I suppose I felt she was right. When you're angry with someone it's hard to see beyond faults like that. But when you're not, you just have to accept them.

We talked about the fact that Mother's letter to them had gone missing. Grand-mère said letters didn't normally go missing. But I explained how bad the British post was.

We had tea and cakes at the apartment. The cakes were on a special tiered dish and were all different. Grand-mère said they came from 'the best *pâtisserie* in Paris'. My favourite was a little strawberry tart with creamy custard under the berries. You know how you sometimes want to leave the pastry? Well, the pastry here was so sweet it was almost the best bit. I also liked the baby eclair (though I wish I'd had chocolate to drink, not coffee) and the millefeuille which means a thousand leaves and probably had about a thousand calories. (I am becoming cake-obsessed.)

When it was almost time to go my grandmother suggested she walk me to the metro and on the way she stopped outside a smart dress shop and made me go in with her. She went over to the sales assistant and they both looked me up and down for a bit. The assistant readjusted the fabric of the floral Oxfam dress round my middle and held my chin so as to study my face in the light. She flicked through the rails and pulled out a pair of brown trousers and a long-sleeved T-shirt top in a sort of plum. They pushed me into the changing rooms and made me try them on. All I could think at first was, 'Oh no, not brown!' which I realize was v. ungrateful of me. Then all I could think was, 'Oh no, too tight.' In fact, I thought that several times because she kept having to bring me larger sizes (I'm obviously deceptive. I don't always look it, but really I'm *grosse comme un éléphant.*) Finally I was standing in the middle of the shop in a pair of trousers that fitted and the plum top, which I thought was too tight (big boobs – yikes), but they announced was perfect.

There was a smile on my grandmother's face that

touched me. She gave me a kiss on the forehead and I felt my eyes fill with tears. She said she'd missed a lot of birthdays and Christmases and this was the least she could do.

Do you see what I mean? She might be a snob, but she's also the kindest person in the world.

💜 *P's bedroom, 6.45 p.m.*

Pascale has just got home. She looks ruffled, as if she's been snogging on the back of a motorbike. Probably because she's been snogging on the back of a motorbike. She told Madame Blanc she was meeting Stéphanie, aka the Crying Girl, but I bet she hooked up with Eric. Her hair looks squashed as if it's been under a helmet.

We're going out tonight. Apparently, there's a party at some friend of Eric's we can go to. I've rung Julie and she's coming with Virginie. I'm not going to ask Delilah. I know it's mean of me, but I want Julie to myself for once. Hopefully D won't find out.

François and the CG will be there, but I'll hide. He's stopped phoning at last and I haven't seen him hovering outside the house for a few days, so I think he's got the message. I think I'll wear my new clothes.

Oh no, I keep forgetting. I must ring Mother to tell her the great news about *mes grandparents*.

💜 94 💜

I've rung Mother. I wish I hadn't.

Mr Spence – I mean John – answered. He said he'd been decorating my room. 'I hope you like shocking pink,' he said. 'I've always seen you as a shocking pink sort of girl.'

I am trying to like him – just because I think he's a twerp with horrible hairy knees doesn't necessarily make him an unsuitable boyfriend for Mother – but this was too much.

'PINK! I'm not a PINK person. How could you think I was a PINK person. I mean PINK is for sparkly little girls like Marie. Or for spoilt princesses like Delilah. PINK! I mean, how could you? What sort of a person would paint another person's bedroom PINK without asking first? I mean, didn't Mother –'

'I'm only joking,' he said in a small voice. 'We went for an off-white. Hint of macaroon.'

'Oh.'

'I'll get Bernadette.'

Mother sounded v. excited to speak to me. 'Oh, Constance, *ma petite* . . . I am so sorry we have been missing each other every time we ring. How is Paris? Are you having a lovely, lovely, lovely time?'

I told her I was. I told her about meeting up with Delilah and Julie, how I'd been to Fontainebleau, how nice the Blancs were (couldn't say anything else as they were in the room). And then I said, 'And . . . you'll never guess, but I've met my grandparents. I, er, bumped into my grandmother and today I went there for tea.'

My voice went high when I said 'tea'. I was trying so hard to sound a) casual and b) jolly. Mother didn't say anything, so I chattered on, filling up the silence.

'Their flat is lovely – they've moved obviously since you last saw them. It's quite small, but full of furniture – and in a very chic *arrondissement*. They were so pleased to meet me. They can't wait to meet Cyril and Marie. And . . . you, of course.'

She still didn't say anything.

'The only odd thing is that they never got your letter saying I was coming.'

'OK . . .'

'Which Grand-mère says is bizarre because the French post system is very good, but then I told her all about how letters in England are always getting lost or taking for ever to get somewhere and –'

'Constance. I didn't send a letter.'

'What do you mean? You said you would.'

'I know, I said, *petite*. But I did not. I tried to write, but . . . It's been a long time. And it has been so painful for me. When your father died, I had no mother's breast to cry upon. I . . . I . . . They are no longer my parents in my heart.'

'But you are still their child. Their only child. They are longing to see you. They say they've tried to get in touch with you, but that you always rebuff them, but that now so much time has passed surely –'

'Constance. That's enough.'

'What do you mean?'

'Constance, I don't want to talk about it. I am glad that you have seen them. I couldn't stop you doing that. But that's enough now. This phone call is costing les Blancs a lot of money, so we will say goodbye. A big kiss from everyone here. OK?'

I hung up feeling small and rebuked. And now I'm really confused. How can somebody be that cross for so many years? When Julie and I have arguments, it might last a week, but it gets boring not being friends. You keep thinking of things you want to tell them and then you remember that you can't. You carry a sort of lump around in your chest, and you can't concentrate on anything else – almost like when you're desperate for a wee. Imagine being desperate for a wee for fifteen years.

❤ *P's bedroom, 7.45 p.m.*

I'm lying on my bed, waiting for Pascale to finish getting ready to go out. I finished ages ago. I've put on my new trousers and top. I can't curl up like I normally would for fear of crumpling my new items. I feel a bit weird. I can't stop thinking about Mother ... Oh, bugger it. I'm going to put her reaction to the back of my mind. Tonight, I'm not Connie Pickles. I'm Constance de Bellechasse.

Pascale, who is looking magnificent tonight, like an angry crow, says I look chic, but . . .

'What?'

Apparently, I need make-up. I didn't bring any so I'm using hers. Will avoid the black lipstick on grounds of taste. Also I don't want to handle stolen goods. On the other hand, all her make-up has probably been stolen somewhere along the way, so maybe I don't have much choice.

Chapter Thirteen

New vocab: un coup de foudre (love at first sight)

Saturday 5 April continued (or rather Sunday 6 April)

❤ *Under the bedclothes, 4 a.m.*

Very, very, very late. Or rather early. Far too late. Or far too early. I can't go to sleep with excitement.

The most amazing thing has happened. Oh, I can hardly write a word. I'm all wobbly inside.

Not Connie Pickles or Constance de Bellechasse, but Madame Constance Blanc.

I've just laughed out loud. I must be careful not to wake the others. (Pascale is in her bed; Julie, Delilah, Virginie and Mimi are in sleeping bags on the floor.) I want to go through every single moment of last night.

So, where was I? Pascale helped me put on some make-up (mascara, sparkly silver eyeshadow, blusher and a plum lipstick) and then we went downstairs to the kitchen.

We were going to go to the party with Philippe, but there was no sign of him. Madame Blanc said he'd gone out. For a moment, a light seemed to go out inside me, but Didier, who was reading the paper at the table, said he'd take us in the car.

He drove us to Champigny, to a weirdly empty flat a couple of streets away from Julie. Eric was already there and he whisked P back out the front door the moment we arrived. Didier seemed to know Etienne, whose flat it was (I think he, Etienne and Eric had been in the same class at school). I thought he was just dropping us off, but he came in. I was quite glad as the only people I recognized were those girls who laughed at me in the bar the night of the François lunge. Oh and buggeration, with them was Stéphanie, the Crying Girl, only she didn't seem to be crying at just that moment. She was a laughing girl. I smiled across the living room and mouthed, 'Ça va?' but she turned away and said something to one of the others and then they all started cackling again. All I can say is I hope she never goes on an English exchange and gets laughed at like that.

'You OK?' Didier was still at my elbow. 'You ignore those idiots,' he said in English. 'They are silly little girls.'

'I'm fine,' I said. 'Julie and Virginie will be here in a

minute. Don't feel you have to stay to look after me.'
To be honest, although I was grateful for his concern,
I was a bit embarrassed standing next to him. I wondered
if he, or his v-neck jumper or the squareness of his
glasses, wasn't the reason the girls were laughing.

'I want to.' He gave me a funny look. (He is the king
of funny looks.) Then he smiled. 'Your hair it's very
good,' he said. 'You are a very pretty girl.'

God! Compliments! A whole new world. Luckily I
didn't have to respond because Julie walked in. First her.
Then Virginie. Then Delilah and Mimi.

Delilah and Mimi?

'Delilah! What are you doing here?'

'Julie invited me. Your hair! It's amazing!'

'Wow. Yes, it's great!' Julie hugged me as if nothing
were wrong. 'Delilah rang to see what we were doing
and I told her to come along. It's OK, isn't it?'

'Of course it is,' I said stiffly. I felt horribly put out.
I hadn't wanted Delilah to come and now she was here
I felt embarrassed at what she might be thinking.

She didn't seem to be upset. 'Where did you get it
done?' she was saying. 'You look like a film star!'

'It's a long story. Hi, Virginie, Mimi.'

'Those strides! Are they Agnès b? They are, aren't
they?' Julie was twisting me round to look at the label
at the back of my trousers. 'And your top! Low cut.
Saucy geezer. And all that make-up. Where did you get
all this stuff?'

Delilah stood back. 'Connie, you look amazing.'

Mimi said, 'Est-ce qu'on a fait des petits achats?' or something. But everyone ignored her.

'Hello, I am Didier, the brother of Pascale.'

Oh, Lordy, I hadn't really wanted to get into all that, but I had to introduce Didier to everyone. Julie mouthed, 'The brother?' when he was talking to Mimi and I mouthed, 'The other one,' back.

I was still feeling odd about Julie having invited Delilah — it means they spoke on the phone without my permission! But I didn't have time to think about it much more. I couldn't sulk, what with ME being the centre of attention.

Later, Pascale and Eric returned to the party — Eric smeared with so much black lipstick it looked like he'd been checking his bike oil with his head. Then they did some mad dancing — like le roc only with extra head-banging. Virginie met someone she knew — one of the laughing girls — and went off into another room. Mimi and Didier struck up some long earnest conversation in French, only occasionally saying something comprehensible like 'Tony Blair' or 'Jean-Claude Van Damme'. And Julie, Delilah and I sat in a corner and I told them in detail about a) my hair, the rise and fall of, b) my visit to my grandparents and shopping trip thereof and c) my conversation with Mother, shock, horror, etc.

'You mean she wasn't pleased?' Delilah looked appalled. (Parents usually do what she expects of them.)

'Not. At. All.'

Julie said, 'Maybe it was just the shock.'

'Maybe,' I agreed. 'But I don't think she's going to be dashing across the Channel to meet them herself, which is what I was hoping.'

'Can't you get her over on false pretences?' I could see I'd caught Julie's interest with this. One thing you can say about Julie: she likes a challenge.

'Like what?'

'I'll put my mind to it.'

The flat was filling up all this time. It had got hot and airless. I was suddenly desperate for water. I told the others I was going to the kitchen and began battling my way through the people in the hallway. I hadn't got far when I heard my name called and turned round to find myself face to face – nose to nose it was so squashed – with François.

'Ahhh,' he said, half closing his eyes and breathing alcohol all over me. 'Constance.' He swayed and put his arm round my neck. 'Constance.' He started nuzzling me even though I was trying to push him away. Sweat was dripping off his nose.

'Get off!' I squealed and tried to get past him, but I couldn't move. I tried to turn back, but as I swivelled I jogged his arm and the bottle of beer he was holding in his spare hand jogged over the boy in a red scarf next to him. He turned round and started shouting. I was trying to say sorry. François was still trying to snog me. And then, suddenly, a strangulated squeal rang in my ears and there was the Crying Girl, who only a few moments ago had been laughing, crying her eyes out again and hitting me with her fists at the same time.

I came to Paris to experience the world, to increase my understanding of other cultures, to broaden my horizons, but honestly.

And then – de de de de-de-da (sound of thundering hooves) – Didier came to my rescue. He pushed François into the kitchen, mopped down the jeans of the boy in the red scarf, pulled the Crying Girl, who had sunk to the floor, to her feet and disappeared with her out of the front door. Delilah and Julie were watching at a safe distance, hooting with laughter. 'What are you like?' Julie cried. 'What's happened to you? Ever since you arrived in Paris you've become a walking disaster.'

'It's like you're creating havoc everywhere you go,' said Delilah, doubled up.

'You're the one who's supposed to get us out of trouble,' continued Julie, wiping her eyes.

'I know,' I said, beginning to laugh myself. 'Let's get out of here before François comes after me. I'll just tell Pascale we'll make our own way home.'

We collected Mimi and Virginie and snuck out to the street – the CG was huddled next to Didier on the garden wall. He gave us a look, which might have been appeal, but which I ignored. (I feel a bit guilty now.) It was only about 9.30 p.m. and the rest of us decided to have a hot chocolate in the cafe near the station.

We were almost there when we bumped into Philippe with a gang of friends.

I said, 'Philippe, *salut!*'

The girls stopped so suddenly they sort of piled into each other like in a cartoon.

Philippe smiled vaguely, and then did a double take. 'Connie!' he said.

I introduced him to M and V, D and J, told him what we were doing and, to all our amazement (well, I know I was amazed and the others stood there with their mouths catching flies, so I think they were too), he waved goodbye to his friends and came to the cafe with us.

What happened next has never happened to me before. I'm usually the one reading my book in the corner. I'm never the one at the centre of the circle, the one everyone else looks at when they're talking. I didn't notice immediately and, when I did, I didn't feel embarrassed, but excited and showy-offy – like Marie when she's doing her ballet in front of the neighbours. I started waving my arms around when I spoke and throwing back my head to laugh. And Philippe sat next to me the whole time, really close, with his leg touching mine, giving me sips of his beer, teasing me about how shy I'd been when he first met me and how red I went when anyone asked me a question and how English I was. Julie and Delilah laughed along with him, even though they're no less English than I am. In fact, they're more English because I'm half French. For once I didn't remind anyone. I liked feeling exotic and kooky and . . . oh, I just liked, LOVED Philippe talking to me.

When we got up to go, he was still next to me and when we walked to the RER, he walked alongside me. And when we got on the train, he sat down opposite me and put out his long, slim legs so the others had to sit on the seats behind. And . . . and . . . I was wittering on, about how the RER differed to the trains you find on Network SouthEast – when he leant across and put his finger to my lips. And then . . . And then, dear reader, he kissed me.

It was only one stop, and the kiss didn't take up most of it. It wasn't wet, like that boy at the summer disco, or breathy like with William, or plunging like with François, it was just velvety. Soft and velvety. He tasted of beer and coffee. He smelt sweet and floral like someone else's washing powder.

(Kiss no. 4: 10/10)

Afterwards I covered my mouth with my hand. The others didn't seem to have noticed. Philippe made a sort of tutting noise and laughed. (Why did he do that? Who was he tutting? Me? Or him? Or maybe it wasn't a tutting. Maybe it was humming.)

When we got to La Varenne, he jumped to his feet and got out of the train boisterously, swinging from the rail and barging through the door. He made us all run down the road to the house. I was a bit disappointed. I thought he'd want to linger behind and kiss me again. But he didn't.

Only one other thing. Before us girls went up to bed (Madame Blanc was very nice in a silent way and sorted the others out with sleeping bags) he passed me on his way into the bathroom and winked.

It was a wink that made my stomach turn somersaults. It was a wink that curled up my toes. It was a wink that sent wild horses careering through my heart.

It was a very nice wink.

He wouldn't wink if he didn't like me, would he?

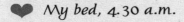 *My bed, 4.30 a.m.*

Just realized I haven't thought about William for fifty-six hours.

Chapter Fourteen

New vocab: *faire la gueule* (to sulk)

Same day
♥ *6 p.m.*

I feel skittish and on edge. I don't know whether to read my book or watch TV. I don't really want to watch TV (a game show modelled on *Who Wants To Be A Millionaire?*) but I can't concentrate on my book because Monsieur Blanc has the volume on v. loud. He's not watching either – he's reading the papers – but he'd grump if I turned it down. I could go upstairs but I don't want to in case ... well, in case Philippe comes back.

So, that's why I'm writing in here.

It's been a really boring day. I've seen Philippe for about three seconds of it. He came into the kitchen when I was making breakfast – after the others had slunk off home – and he winked at me! He wouldn't wink at me unless he cared, would he?

We went to church this morning – very long and tedious and might as well have been in Latin for all I understood. Philippe didn't go, but the rest of us had to. I sat next to Didier and managed to whisper thank you for rescuing me from the Crying Girl. He said it was his pleasure. 'Where did you go after that?' he said, looking a bit hurt.

Lunch was potatoes, chicken and green beans – not together but separate, in that order. Afterwards when Monsieur Blanc was mowing the grass – going up and down in neat grumpy rows – Madame Blanc put on her mac, said something about seeing the priest and went out. She looked shifty, I thought; pink around the eyes. I wonder if she had some extra confessions to make. And, if so, what. She has been even quieter over the last few days than usual. I haven't even seen her talking to Didier. And when Monsieur Blanc shouted at her this morning for not having bought a fresh baguette in time for breakfast, her face had a closed, shuttered look to it. I wonder if she's ill. Maybe she has a terrible incurable disease she is keeping from the family, and that was why she was visiting the pipe-smoking doctor and that is why he kissed her. In sympathy. Oh, poor Madame Blanc. I don't think I can bear to think about it.

This afternoon Pascale suggested we go to some

shopping centre further out of Paris. I didn't want to go out in case Philippe came home. In the end, she and Eric went bowling and I just hung around the house, eating my way through a bag of *madeleines* (yummy little sweet cakes) we bought in the *boulangerie* after church, playing the occasional game of cards with Didier and trying not to be noticed by Monsieur B.

I keep thinking, would he have gone out all day if he felt the same for me as I do for him?

♥ Living room, 7 p.m.

Philippe has just flown into the house and flown out again. A group of his friends waited for him outside the front door. Before he flew off, he called, '*Grand bisou*,' to me and Pascale. I've looked it up in my dictionary. It means big kiss.

Oh, hope!

♥ Still living room, 10 p.m.

I'm feeling v. tired. I don't think I can stay up much longer. And it wouldn't be cool if he discovered I'd been waiting for him. Maybe I don't look very nice today. Perhaps I should have worn the lipstick and the clothes.

A bad day. Oh, woe.

Chapter Fifteen

New vocab: *Il m'aime. Il ne m'aime pas. Il m'aime. Il ne m'aime pas.* (He loves me. He loves me not. He loves me. Etc.)

Monday 7 April

💜 *10 a.m.*

I've *spoken to* Julie on the phone. We're meeting for a hot chocolate in the bar in Champigny.

💜 *RER platform, waiting for train back, 11.45 a.m.*

Julie can't believe Philippe kissed me! I told her everything. I almost got over my disappointment at the way he treated me yesterday in reliving the moment.

'But when?' she kept saying.

'On the RER.'

'But we were there too.'

'You were behind us.'

'But I'd have noticed.'

'It was,' it pained me to admit it, 'very quick.'

'But he's GORGEOUS.'

'I know. I know.' Getting quieter and more resigned every time. 'I know.'

She asked if I'd told Delilah and when I said I hadn't, she got out her mobile phone and began dialling her. 'She'll love it. She'll love it,' she was saying. I had to wrest the phone from between her fingers and threaten to drop it into her hot choc.

'I don't *want* you telling Delilah,' I said. 'She doesn't have to know everything I do.'

Julie raised her eyebrows. 'What's up?'

'I didn't know you even liked her.'

'Didn't you?'

'She can be so . . . selfish, can't she, and spoilt?' I was being disloyal and bitchy.

'I know. But, well, she's different over here. She's funny. But listen, back to Philippe – the well-fit Philippe. What happened yesterday? Did he do it again? Has he been all over you ever since?'

'NO.' I forgot Delilah and told Julie how he'd barely registered my existence since Saturday night. She thought he might be playing it cool. Or that maybe he hasn't been feeling very well. Or that perhaps he is waiting for more of a cue from me.

'Perhaps he's shy,' she said.

'Do you think so?'

'Yeah. Or . . .'

'What?'

'Maybe he just doesn't fancy you.'

I looked so stricken she laughed and said of course he did or he wouldn't have kissed me in the first place. I went on about it quite a lot more, but by the time I'd provided about fifteen different interpretations for the wink, I detected a slight glazing in the eye region and shut up.

We moved on to other matters. Julie's decided the Leboeufs are not poisoning her, though she does wish Virginie was a bit more fun. She's very keen on horses. 'Nuff said,' Julie added darkly.

We talked a bit about Karl – she read out his texts (yawn) and then we got on to Mother and her parents. Julie got all efficient, just as she did when I was trying to find Mother a boyfriend the other month, and started listing possible stratagems for bringing her to Paris.

1. Fake illness

It would have to be serious, possibly life-threatening, to guarantee her arrival. This would be a) hard to pull off convincingly and b) a little on the cruel side – mothers generally being quite liable to health-related panics.

2. Free holiday

Organize some sort of competition/prize draw in which Mother wins two tickets to Paris and a night in a hotel – reservations couriered to her door in a manner she can't refuse. (The problems with this are mainly finance-related. Like, where are we going to get the money for the tickets. And the hotel. And the courier.)

3. Mobilize Mr Spence

Now we're talking. Mr Spence, the old romantic, is definitely a hidden resource. As soon as I get back I'm going to tap him.

❤ 12.30 p.m.

Phone call to home as follows:

Marie, who answered: 'It's Connie. It's Connie. It's Connie. Connie, guess what, I'm going to LEGOLAND this weekend. Daddy's taking me. But he's not taking Cyril because he threw his bacon sandwich on the floor when Granny Enid made it specially and then he kicked me and I didn't do anything.'

(Cyril, in background: 'I am coming to LEGOLAND. And you started it. You're not going to LEGOLAND. And I hate bacon. I hate the white bits. They're disgusting. They're like worms.')

Marie: 'You're like worms.'

Me: 'Marie, sweetie. Lovely to catch up and everything, but is Jack there?'

Jack: 'What do you want? Money?'

Me: 'Ha. Ha. No, can you look after Marie and Cyril all weekend?'

Jack: 'Yeah, no : . . I have just met this new girl, fabulous . . . works in telesales . . . very keen on fruit, thinking Saturday night –'

Me, warningly: 'Jack?'

Jack: 'Yes, Connie. I can look after Marie and Cyril all weekend.'

Me: 'Good. Can you get Mr Spence down from my bedroom please.'

Mr Spence, doubtful: 'Constance? How are you?'

Me: 'Just ringing to check how the shocking pink is coming along.'

Mr Spence, anxious: 'Er . . . hint of macaroon, remember.'

Me: 'I know. Only joking. But listen. I've had a wonderful thought. Mother. French. Hasn't been to Paris for fifteen years. Paris. City of love, of romance. Minibreaks. The perfect way to get to know your lover. The perfect escape. Easter. Coming up. Perfect timing. Marie and Cyril. Lovely kids. Lovely to escape from. Mr Spence – John – what do you say?'

I think he got what I was getting at. He started laughing halfway through. 'What do you want?' he said. 'Money?'

'No,' I shrieked indignantly. 'I just want Mother to be happy. You to be happy.'

'Yes . . . ?'

'Oh, and I'm a bit homesick. If I know she's coming next weekend – and she won't come unless dragged – then I'll have something to look forward to. And, oh yeah, I met my grandmother. We could all meet up when you come to Paris, but better not tell Mum – let's make it a nice surprise.'

He sounded convinced by this and then he started getting excited. He's never been to Paris himself. Imagine that! A grown man and everything. 'I'd love to go to Paris,' he said. 'Notre Dame. The Eiffel Tower. I bet it's quite something, the Eiffel Tower. Is it?'

'Er. I don't exactly know. I haven't exactly seen it. Yet.'

'Oh.'

I'm going to have to leave it in his paint-splattered hands for the moment. And now I can hear Philippe in the hall – oh, yikes – so I'm going to stop writing in here, go downstairs and hover, looking interesting.

♥ *Under the bedclothes, 9 p.m.*

What have I done wrong? Philippe hardly looked at me all through supper. It's as if nothing has happened. Is it that he's embarrassed in front of his family? I wish I knew. I can't bear it. I think my heart will break.

Chapter Sixteen

New vocab: the old rendezvous va va voom (ask
Mr Spence)

Tuesday 8 April
♥ *P's bedroom, 10 a.m.*

I wish I'd never embarked on this falling-in-love thing.
It's ridiculous. I should stick to books and stationery.
Boys are just a waste of time, emotion and heartbreak.
First there was William, who ruined my life by kissing
me and then going out with my next-door neighbour.
And now there is Philippe, who ruined my life by kissing
me and then IGNORING ME.

Julie has just rung 'to check on proceedings'. She
really meant Mother and Mr Spence, I'm sure. I filled
her in quickly and then wittered on about P. She's very
wise, is Julie. She said in her experience (quite extensive

if we're being honest) boys often lose interest if girls seem too keen.

'Have you seemed too keen, Con?'

'I suppose taking off my clothes and tiptoeing into his bedroom last night with a rose between my teeth might have been *un peu de trop*.'

'Er, Con . . . ?'

'BUT I DIDN'T DO THAT. I went to bed and wept silently under the covers.'

I don't think Pascale knows anything is up. She's going through an ignoring-me phase. I haven't done anything to annoy her, as such. I guess she's just fed up with me being here all the time.

Didier is being nice to me, but then he always is. He's a nice boy. Unlike his horrible brother.

Philippe is *so* horrible.

I wish he'd kiss me again.

I went for a walk by myself earlier, down to the market, and I kept imagining what might happen if I bumped into him, how glad he would be to see me alone, how he would stroke my hair and say we had to be secretive, how he'd promised his father never to marry an English girl, but now he'd met me . . .

Of course I didn't bump into him. Though I did see Madame Blanc in the distance. She was going into the door between the *pharmacie* and the shoe shop, carrying a large suitcase. What on earth is she up to now?

The sun has come out at last. We're so delighted we're acting as if the queen – or as we're in France, the president – has come to visit. Didier lugged the green plastic garden furniture from the shed at the side of the house on to the lawn. It's a small, dark garden, edged on two sides by tall, dark-green trees. Madame Blanc made a jug of lemonade and she carried it outside on a tray. And Pascale put on a skirt! A denim one – it looks nice with her biker's boots. I realize I've never seen her pins. She has a sort of rash on the back of her calves. She saw me looking and said, 'I hate my legs.'

'They're nice,' I said. 'You've got good legs. You shouldn't hide them all the time.'

She went bright red and tried to pull the skirt down. 'My father says I'm fat.'

'You're not fat!'

'I am.'

'You're not.'

'I am.'

'I'm fat.'

'You're not.'

We both laughed.

I've just found out what the rash is. She picks at her skin. She finds an ingrowing hair and, when she's not thinking, she fiddles and pokes it until she makes the skin sore. She's doing it now. That girl is a bundle of nerves.

You'll notice I haven't mentioned Philippe. I haven't seen him all day.

♥ The garden, 2 p.m.

Philippe appeared for lunch. He sat next to me on the grass and I tried to eat really neatly so I wouldn't look gross. He didn't say anything to me directly, but when he'd finished his sandwich he leant across and took something – a leaf, I think – out of my hair.

I felt a charge of electricity between us. I thought, he's going to ask me out. But he jumped up and said he was going to the cinema with some friends.

Madame Blanc, who was clearing away the tray, said, 'On a lovely day like this?'

But Pascale jumped to her feet. 'Take us. Take us,' she pleaded.

I crossed my fingers and hoped.

He just laughed. 'You're too young,' he said.

Sob.

♥ The garden, 4 p.m.

Delilah has just rung. I haven't spoken to her since Sunday.

'Just to let you know, I'm off to the south of France,' she said. 'Carol and Bob, Mimi's mum and dad, have a yacht at Nice.'

'Nice,' I said.

'One of Mimi's friends from school is joining us. Then the three of us are flying back – alone – and we're going to spend the weekend in the apartment with only the Filipino housekeeper in charge. So . . . you know what that means.'

'No.'

'Paa-arty.'

'Are you sure?' I said. 'With all their lovely linen sofas and oak antiques?'

'It'll be fine.'

'Just like yours.' Delilah, home alone in London recently, threw a party. The next day her parents' house looked like the bed of the Thames at low tide.

'Exactly,' she said, missing any sarcasm altogether. 'Julie's coming.'

'Oh, is she?' I felt a stab of jealousy.

'And I've been trying to persuade Will to come. I said I'd pay. Mum gave me extra dosh for the holiday so I haven't even touched this month's allowance. But he's such a meany. He said he'd feel out of place. I said, "Aren't you desperate to see me?" He said he could wait another six days. Do you think he still likes me?'

'Of course he does,' I said flatly.

'Anyway, better go. Pascale can come on the condition she doesn't nick anything and she brings her sexy brothers. Got to go. Love ya.'

'Love ya,' I said back.

After I'd hung up, I thought hard about Delilah. She didn't ask me a single question in that phone call. If she had, I might have told her about Philippe, or she might have guessed, from my tone, that something was up. She is really nice and everything, but friendship with Delilah is quite one-sided. You can't hate her for it. Sometimes I think it would be easier if I could.

I'd just come back out to the garden and the phone went again. This time it was Mr Spence. He sounded as if he was on amphetamines. 'We're in business,' he hissed. 'I haven't told Marie and Cyril the details in case they let slip. I haven't told anyone. All Bernadette knows is that it's a mystery tour. Having Jack on board helped. She tried to say she couldn't leave Marie and Cyril but we overruled her. They had some trip to LEGOLAND planned anyway. He's got a new girlfriend in telesales . . . enough of that. I've got a last-minute three-day package off the Internet. We're staying in the Best Western – four stars! Right by the Champs Elysées. We are talking boats being pushed out.' He gave a geeky laugh. 'Anyway, we get there Friday night. I'm thinking we might meet up with you then, get acclimatized, that sort of thing. Saturday, leave us to it, and then Sunday, when we're hunky and dory, you organize the old rendezvous va va voom with the old parents.'

'Va va voom?' I said.

'Constance. I'm excited. Give an old man a break.'

He's funny like that, Mr Spence. Just when you have him down as a complete idiot, he surprises you by being quite approachable.

And give him his due. He had a mission and he's done it!

💜 *P's bedroom, 6 p.m.*

I've just rung my grandmother to tell her about Mother's arrival this weekend.

She said, 'Bernadette, coming here?'

'Yes.'

'Where?'

'To Paris.'

'Here? To Paris?'

'YES!'

There was a long silence in which I think I heard her crying. Then she said, 'But that is fantastic, incredible. Will she stay with us? Will she come here straight from the train? Shall we pick her up at the Gare du Nord?'

I had to tell her to hold her horses, that we still had a little way to go. 'But don't you worry,' I said. 'Connie Pickles, aka Constance de Bellechasse, is on the case.'

Chapter Seventeen

New swearwords: *une garce* (a bitch); *une salope* (a tart); *une vache* (a cow)

Wednesday 9 April
❤ *Bathroom, 8 p.m.*

I'm hiding up here but I can't stay long. This is the first chance I've had to write all day. There is nowhere to go in this house. Even though my home is always full of people, at least I've got my own space, and the roof to climb on to if it's not raining.

Dreadful things have been happening here. Pascale has locked herself in her room. Philippe has stormed out into the night – well, the evening. And Didier and Monsieur Blanc are pacing up and down in the living room. We haven't had any supper. The phone keeps ringing. The front door keeps banging. The police have been and gone. Monsieur Blanc's sister will be arriving any minute. I wish I could make myself really, really small because then I could slip down the plughole and stay there until it's all over.

Madame Blanc has left Monsieur Blanc.

It began as an ordinary day. Pascale slept in until 11 a.m. and I read my book in the garden, sipping hot chocolate and hoping Philippe would come out and talk to me. (He didn't.)

Madame Blanc was busy in the kitchen, cooking up enormous vats of what turned out to be several family meals, now stacked in the freezer. I did offer to help, but she shook her head and flashed me a smile – like a light being switched on and off. I didn't think much of it. She's never very friendly to me. I used to think it was embarrassment at not being able to speak any English, but now I think maybe she never wanted me to be here. I'm just one more thing, like the enormous flat-screen television, that her husband has brought into the house against her wishes.

At about 10.45 a.m., she started washing up. But she didn't just wash the pans she'd been using. She washed every single plate in the cupboard, every saucepan on the shelf, every knife and fork in the drawer. Then she got out the vacuum cleaner – which woke Pascale and led to a lot of screaming, which Madame B ignored – and vacuumed the house from top to toe. Then, still not speaking to anyone, she laid the table for lunch. A plate of cold meats, a baguette and a dish of gherkins were left under tea towels on the sideboard. And then she put on her mac, slung her handbag over her shoulder, and walked out of the front door. She didn't say goodbye to anyone. And she didn't look back.

None of us really noticed she wasn't back for lunch. We just thought she was at the supermarket. If Monsieur Blanc had been there it might have been different. But he had left very early to furnish some hotel in Versailles. Nobody sat down properly anyway, just sort of picked when they felt hungry. I wasn't even thinking about Madame B. I was too busy watching Philippe, checking my tummy wasn't hanging out over the waistband of my new trousers, keeping tabs on the crumbs around my mouth and the salami fat between my teeth, making sure I was laughing at the right things, that I was paying enough attention to Philippe for my feelings to be obvious, but not paying so much attention that they were too obvious. It was all quite hard work.

Didier asked if there was any sight in Paris I was still longing to see and I said, darting a look at Philippe, 'The Eiffel Tower! I'd love to go up the Eiffel Tower!' and Didier said, as it was a nice afternoon, maybe we should go. 'All of us?' I said brightly, hardly bearing to look at Philippe.

Who knows whether he would have come or not, because it was about then that Monsieur Blanc arrived home. He was due back this evening, but there had been some problem with the hotel wardrobes that he had to sort out this end. He seemed annoyed that lunch had been eaten without him and shouted for Thérèse. 'Is there no soup?' he said to us when she didn't come. His eyes were bloodshot and spittle collected at the corners of his mouth.

Pascale and Didier disappeared into the kitchen to try and rustle some up. Philippe sat down next to Monsieur B and they engaged in a jolly banter that went over my head. It's funny – Philippe doesn't seem to notice what a bully he is and has a much easier ride as a result. When P and D scurried back in with a plate of watercress soup they'd warmed up from a packet, all they got was abuse: 'It's too cold,' he said, and shoved it to the other side of the table.

He had to make a lot of phone calls after lunch and it wasn't until 4 p.m. that he went upstairs to change out of his suit. I know that because Didier looked at his watch and said, 'Is it too late for the Eiffel Tower?' And Pascale said, noticing for the first time, 'I wonder where Mum is.' She didn't have to wonder for long because there was a bellow from upstairs – the sort of sound, tortured and angry, that a sumo wrestler emits just before he lunges.

Monsieur Blanc stormed back down the stairs, shouting and swearing. You couldn't get much sense out of him. He was half changed, wearing his work trousers, socks and a vest. 'In the bedroom. The bedroom!' he hollered at one point. Didier exchanged glances with Pascale and then went upstairs himself. He came back down, holding a note.

Madame Blanc had left. She had had enough of being an unpaid servant in her own home. She was sorry to do it to the children but for the first time in her life she was putting herself before anyone else. She didn't say where she was going and she left no forwarding address. She said she would be in touch in a few days.

Her half of the wardrobe was empty.

When Monsieur Blanc began shouting, my instinct was to escape, but the moment Didier read the note out, Pascale started sobbing so I stayed to comfort her. Philippe went into the garden. We could hear him whistling. When he came back in, he said he had some friends to meet and left the house. (Poor lamb – I think he was covering how upset he was.) It was left to Didier to try and calm his father down. He was still raging. Where was she? Where had she gone? Who would know? Who could he ring?

The awful thing is that no one could think of anyone. If Madame Blanc had friends, none of her family knew who they were.

It was then he decided she'd been abducted and rang the police. While we were waiting for them, he calmed down a bit. Didier went upstairs and got him a shirt and some shoes and persuaded him to sit still for a few moments on the sofa. Pascale, who had stopped crying, made some coffee, which we forced him to drink. Monsieur Blanc, seeing me, said, 'So, mothers and wives, they behave like this in England, do they?'

I said I thought, maybe, they behaved like this everywhere, which was The Wrong Answer.

'What do you mean? Are you telling me she has a
right to leave her home, her family? Are you telling me
I should let her just walk out and –'

'Ssh, Papa.' Didier put his hand on his arm. Monsieur
Blanc went quiet again.

The police didn't stay long. Didier showed them the
note and they made their excuses and sidled off to find
a real crime elsewhere.

Didier rang Monsieur Blanc's sister, who lives in
Nancy, and she is driving over. Eric came round and I
can see him out of the window, sitting on the front
wall, giving Pascale a hug.

❤ *My bed, 11 p.m.*

I'm going to write very quietly because it's silent in the
house at last.

Valérie Blanc arrived at 9 p.m. She is tall and blonde
and has much softer features than her brother, although
she has the same beaked nose. Didier told me she has
an import business, distributing Moroccan artefacts –
decorated straw bags, leather slippers, beaded belts – to
boutiques in France. She's older than Monsieur Blanc,
but much more glamorous.

She took one look at Monsieur Blanc and threw her
arms round him. 'My poor little brother,' she said. Poor?
Little? It's funny to think of someone having that sort

of relationship with him, to think that she feels for him in the same way that I feel for Cyril.

She ran him a bath, poured him a big glass of wine and went out to HyperCasino to buy two ready-cooked chickens and some fresh bread. When we were all sitting around the table (I say 'all', but Philippe still hadn't come home) she said, 'Right. What has been going on? Which of you has driven my sister-in-law from the house?'

She was joking, but only sort of. Monsieur Blanc was staring down at the table. He hadn't eaten anything. I said, trying to be light-hearted, 'Maybe me? Maybe it's the extra work, all the cooking, the cleaning, the beds . . .'

'It's certainly true she had to put up with four of your friends sleeping over last weekend.' Didier was joking too, but again only sort of. It hadn't crossed my mind until then that it might have been an imposition. I said, 'Oh yes. Oh God, I'm sorry. Oh God.'

'Don't be ridiculous.' Monsieur Blanc looked up and there was so much anger in his face I wished I hadn't said anything. 'It's not you. It's nobody here but me. It's me, I tell you.'

'Calm down.' Valérie put her hand on his. 'Eat. Drink. Then go to bed. Tomorrow is a new day. Jean? Pascale? Didier? Do any of you have any idea where Thérèse might have gone? Nobody has seen her? No. Well, tomorrow we will be detectives. Tomorrow we will find out.'

💜 *Under the bedclothes,* 11.30 p.m.

I've just remembered something. I saw Madame Blanc going into that apartment above the shoe shop. Then I saw her taking her suitcase there. And I saw her kissing the man with the pipe.

I'm not going to tell anyone. Monsieur Blanc might kill her.

💜 *Still under,* 11.35 p.m.

I don't suppose I'm ever going to go up the Eiffel Tower.

Chapter Eighteen

New vocab: *la petite amie* (a girlfriend); *la petite fille* (a young daughter)

Thursday 10 April
♥ *9 a.m.*

Monsieur Blanc is in his pyjamas at the dining-room table, demanding embraces from all of his children. Pascale is sitting next to him and stroking his hand. His normally neat beard is ragged. His eyes are bloodshot. His lips are chapped. Occasionally he puts his head into his hands and sobs. 'I love her,' he cries. 'She is the only woman for me.' I think he is drunk.

'There, there.' Valérie puts another tot of brandy in his *café*. 'We'll find her. Never you mind.'

💜 *Living room, 10 a.m.*

Philippe, a vision of total hunkdom today in faded jeans and a white cap-sleeved T-shirt, has news. Monique, his 'little friend' (friend? Girlfriend? Oh God. Why am I still having such thoughts at a time like this?) saw Madame Blanc going into the shoe shop at 4.20 p.m. yesterday afternoon. Philippe told Didier who told me. I pretended to look surprised. The two of them are going to sneak out and investigate. I'm going to go with them.

💜 *Living room, 10.20 a.m.*

Monsieur Blanc is still weeping at the dining-room table.

💜 *The garden, 12 noon*

When we walked into the shoe shop, the assistant was serving the woman from the *boulangerie* – who was still in her white apron – and getting down boxes of Scholl sandals for her to try on. Didier was very polite. He just said, '*Bonjour, Madame,*' and stood by the till. But Philippe stood next to her, talking impatiently. 'We are looking for our mother,' he said. 'She came in here yesterday. Four twenty. Tell me the truth. We have a witness.'

The shoe lady looked at him and looked away again. She said she had served a lot of customers yesterday. She could not remember 4.20 p.m., but if he were to wait for a few instants she would look on the till.

Then she and the woman from the *boulangerie* talked quickly and angrily between themselves – I could tell from their tone they were berating Philippe. But he is so rude! Who does he think he is coming in here and shouting at her! She has worked in La Varenne for nine years and never before . . . ! The young today!

Finally the *boulangerie* woman paid and left, casting outraged glances at Philippe over her shoulder. The shoe lady went to the till and fiddled about without saying anything. Eventually she looked up. 'I did serve a customer yesterday at four fifteen. A Monsieur de Valois. Is that whom you are looking for?'

Didier smiled. He put out his hand to shake hers. He said, 'Madame. Thank you so much for your assistance. I don't think Monsieur de Valois is who we are looking for. I'm sorry. We should have introduced ourselves earlier. I am Didier Blanc; this is my brother, Philippe Blanc, and our friend Constance Pickles from England.'

'From England . . . ?' Her eyes lit up.

I smiled encouragingly.

Didier went on. 'Our mother is missing and –'

'Let's go!' Philippe was standing by the door, rattling the handle impatiently. 'She doesn't know anything.'

'Our mother is missing – Madame Blanc – and we

were hoping you might be able to cast some light on this mystery. We are all – her little daughter especially – very upset by her disappearance. We believe she was here yesterday. She has light brown hair. She was wearing . . .'

'A beige mac,' I said.

The shoe-shop lady looked away. She wouldn't meet any of our eyes. 'I'm sorry about your little sister . . .' she began. 'No, I'm sorry. I can tell you no more.'

'She definitely knows something,' Didier said the moment we were on the street.

'Let me go back. I'll get it out of her.'

Philippe was pushing against the door, but Didier held his arm.

'No. It won't do any good. Not now.'

I could see the shoe lady through the window. She was on the telephone, twisting the wire in her fingers, casting panicked looks in our direction.

I said, 'Maybe we should let your mother be? It's what she wants.'

But Philippe said it wasn't fair on their father. They all needed to KNOW. Didier said he just wanted to talk to her. We had started walking down the street and as we passed the *boulangerie*, there was a flutter among the women behind the counter like a line of starlings on a telephone wire. And we hadn't got much further down the road when another woman, younger than the one who bought the Scholls, came out of the shoe shop.

She called to Didier. 'Didier Blanc! I know what you're looking for! It is not for me to tell tales, but if I were you I would ask at l'*auto-école*.'

'L'*auto-école*?' I said. 'What's that?'

'The driving school,' replied Didier.

'Has she been learning to drive?'

'She's been driving for twenty-five years,' Philippe snapped. (A sabre through my heart.)

'I've been learning to drive. It's where I've just had my lessons,' said Didier. 'It's worth a try. Let's go.'

We doubled back on ourselves, up to the RER station, past the HyperCasino supermarket, to the driving school. A young woman in a gypsy top with tightly curled long hair was chewing the end of a biro at the desk. 'Leave it to me,' hissed Didier. He went up to the woman and smiled. He said, 'Véronique, hello. Have you recovered from me, le *monstre* of the roads? Can you believe they passed me? Neither can I!'

She smiled and they chattered for a bit until Didier said, 'Is Michel here?' and very quickly, almost before he'd managed to ask, she said, 'Non. Non. Non. Michel is out. He is out . . . teaching someone to drive! Yes, that's it. He's teaching someone to drive.'

'Well,' Didier laughed breezily, 'it is a driving school. He is a driving instructor. Teaching someone to drive is what he does. Well, then, send him my regards.'

We left and stood outside on the pavement. Didier said Michel, who ran the driving school, was a nice man who kept himself to himself. Shy, thoughtful . . .

He trailed off and added that he thought Véronique had been behaving oddly.

Philippe said she was an odd girl anyway. 'Did you see the state of the biro?' he said.

I didn't say anything, but I'd noticed something: on the desk was an ashtray. And on the ashtray was an upturned pipe.

We were still standing there, lost for a moment, when a car — a red Honda — pulled up and then pulled off again, as if the driver had misread the address. Didier did a double take. 'Hey! That was Michel,' he said. 'What's he . . .'

'There's someone in the car with him!' yelled Philippe, beginning to chase the car down the road to the lights. 'A woman!' The lights changed. The red Honda turned the corner and disappeared. 'Damn!' He limped back. 'I've twisted my ankle.'

I bent to rub it for him. It was probably a stupid, obvious thing to do, but I was on my knees before I could stop myself. He was wearing white tennis socks. 'Poor you,' I said as I stood up. He was looking at me. I thought he might be about to cry. 'Poor you,' I said again.

'You'll live,' Didier said.

'It really hurts.' Philippe was still looking at me. He was biting the corner of his mouth. There was a smear of dirt on his neck and on his white T-shirt.

'Come on. Let's get a coffee.'

Didier pushed us across the road, Philippe leaning

on me, hobbling, into the pizzeria and ordered us all coffee. I'd have preferred hot chocolate, but I didn't like to make a fuss. 'It's mysterious,' Didier said. 'What's she doing this for?'

'Maybe she wants to give Papa a shock,' said Philippe. He'd sat down on the side of the table next to me. He was resting his foot on the seat of my chair. I had to inch away to stop my bum from squashing it.

'Or maybe she's just left,' I said.

They both gave murmurs of agreement. I suddenly realized I was enjoying myself. I was in Paris, in the middle of someone else's crisis, managing to muddle along in French. I felt part of something. *And* I was with two boys that I liked (one of them rather a lot). And if Philippe didn't like me as much as I liked him, if he wasn't going to kiss me again, then I wasn't going to die. In fact it struck me sitting there that sometimes it is almost enough just to know there is someone out there you really like – it makes the world seem full of possibilities. I realize this isn't what Delilah, with her talk of The One, believes. But for me, for now, it will do. (Having said all that, if he doesn't kiss me again, I think I will die.)

'THE RED HONDA!' Didier interrupted my thoughts by jumping to his feet.

The red Honda was pulling up outside the pizzeria. It was parked illegally and the couple inside appeared to be arguing. The passenger door opened and out got Madame Blanc.

The three of us sat and stared.

'Here she is,' said Didier, but nobody moved.

She was looking at us. The red Honda drove off. She opened the door of the pizzeria and walked purposefully towards our corner. She was carrying a supermarket plastic bag. She reached us. Didier stood up and she embraced him.

Philippe said, 'I can't get up – I've twisted my ankle.'

'Poor thing.' She said he needed arnica and there was some in the bathroom cabinet.

'*Bonjour*, Constance,' she said, looking at me levelly. I asked if she wanted me to leave, but she said it was OK for me to stay where I was. She wasn't staying long. She talked quickly so the boys wouldn't interrupt her. She said she'd heard they were looking for her – she did not wish to be the object of a detective trail. She had not run away from her children for ever. But she needed some time. 'I have met someone and I am happy,' she said. 'I am embarking upon a new life.'

I couldn't help noticing the plastic bag she was holding contained cleaning products.

'Is it Michel?' asked Didier.

'Or Véronique?' added Philippe, giggling inappropriately.

'It is Michel,' she said, ignoring Philippe. 'We met on several occasions when, Didier, you were learning to drive. I found him very sympathetic. And he has offered me his heart.'

We sat there, digesting this fact in silence for a few seconds.

Didier said, 'Papa called the police out.'

'No!'

'Yes. But it's OK. They went. Aunt Valérie is here instead.'

'Valérie! In my house?' She looked annoyed for a moment. 'Is he all right, your father?'

Neither Philippe nor Didier answered. She turned to me. I shrugged.

'What do you mean?' She imitated my shrug.

'I mean, not really.'

'Not really? I thought he might be ... relieved.'

'Relieved?' Didier gave a hollow laugh. 'He is devastated. You can start your new life, but know that he is devastated.'

'Truly?' She glanced in anguish from one son to the other. When they didn't answer, she tucked her hair behind her ears, smoothed her skirt and said, 'Well, I am surprised. Here ...' She wrote something down on a piece of paper and handed it to Didier. 'You can phone me on this number if you need me. Now, *au revoir*.' She stood up and kissed all six of our cheeks and then she was gone.

❤ *The garden, 3 p.m.*

The boys made a pact on the way home that they wouldn't tell Pascale or their father about the meeting with their mother. They don't want to upset Pascale and they're scared of what their father might do. They think there is more pleading to be done.

When we got back, Pascale had made lunch – lamb cutlets and salad – and had laid the table in the garden. Valérie had gone out to collect a consignment of Moroccan tea lights.

While we were eating, Monsieur Blanc kept telling Pascale how delicious the meal was and how clever a little cook she was, which was nice. 'Of course, you get it from your mother,' he said. 'She is a fantastic cook.' And then he launched into a long reminiscence about how they first met: how she had been going out with a friend of his and they had got together at a picnic in the Bois de Boulogne and she had made this wild-boar pâté: '. . . the deliciousness, the freshness, oh, to meet a girl who made her own wild-boar pâté . . .'

Didier and I exchanged several glances through this until finally he said: 'Papa, I don't think Mother realizes how much you love and appreciate her. I wonder if – when – she comes back, you should not be angry with her, but tell her all the things you've been telling us.'

Monsieur Blanc seemed to recover himself at this point and made some gruff noises, which prompted the rest of us to clear the table and do the washing-up.

I was doing the glasses when the phone went and everybody jumped. Monsieur Blanc got there first. His face crumpled. 'Constance!' he called irritably. 'For you.'

It was Mr Spence, calling to finalize arrangements for the weekend. Mother doesn't have a clue where she's going. He's told her it's romantic. 'And no bikini required! Ha, ha.'

'Yes, all right,' I said.

We agreed that I'll pick them up from the station and spend a bit of time with them tomorrow. And then we'll meet for lunch, with grandparents, on Sunday.

I rang my grandmother, who is giddy with excitement and obsessed with getting the place right. She ran through several brasseries – this one too crowded, this one too smoky, this one too booked up. In the end, we agreed on somewhere at the top of the Pompidou Centre. 'Are you sure we shouldn't tell Bernadette that we will be there?' she asked anxiously. 'Wouldn't it be better if she was prepared?'

I told her forewarned was forearmed and we didn't want that.

I'm going to write to William now. Unaccountably, despite all that's happening, I miss him.

Chapter Nineteen

New vocab: *une famille française typique* (a typical French family)

Friday 11 April

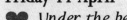 *Under the bedclothes,* 9.30 a.m.

It's Good Friday, the day you should spend contemplating your sins, looking deeply into the darkness of your soul etc., etc. We're going to church this evening, but I'm not going to confession because I can't handle it in French. So, I'll take a moment here to unburden.

1. Technically I am still coveting someone else's property, i.e. William.
2. Unpure thoughts, i.e. Philippe.
3. Deceitful actions. Mother is, even as I write, on the Eurostar. No panicked phone call from Mr Spence,

so he obviously persuaded her on to it. The real sin is arranging Sunday lunch, but I'm sure the Lord knows it is all for her own good.

I'd better go downstairs and see what the mood is today.

💙 *Kitchen, 10 a.m.*

Monsieur Blanc is wearing the dark blue suit he wears for work, with a pale yellow tie. He hasn't done anything about his beard, so he looks like one of those games Marie used to like so much – when you can flick a page and put a different body on the wrong face. He's Monsieur Businessman underneath, the Old Man of the Sea on top.

Valérie has got him helping her with her accounts – they are laid out over the table and he is sitting at the head, tapping on a calculator. She keeps sidling up to tell him how clever he is. It's all a bit care in the community for my liking.

Philippe is at the front door with Pascale and Eric. I went out to see what they were up to. The sky was blue with heavy white clouds. The sun was going in and out. Eric was trying to persuade Pascale to go for a ride with him on his bike. Pascale, who was wearing black eyeliner and a dressing gown, was telling him she couldn't leave her father. Philippe, in long baggy shorts and a vest T-shirt, said, 'I'll come,' and wrapped his arms round Eric from behind and made a slightly obscene hip movement. Eric pulled away and pretended to clobber him and then Pascale started shouting at Philippe. Valérie came out of the house and told them to quieten down. And then Monsieur Blanc emerged and said, 'My daughter, come and quench your poor deserted father's loneliness,' (or something) and Pascale, throwing a defiant look in the direction of her brother and beau, went back into the house with him. Valérie followed.

Eric, who hasn't said a word to me in the fortnight I've been here, flicked his fringe behind his ears and said, 'Do you want to come for a ride?' I didn't really fancy all that grease in my face so I said no and he roared off, leaving me – alone, at last! – with Philippe.

Oh. Oh. Oh.

We sat on the wall and talked! He was so sweet. He said, 'So, you've been here seven whole days now.'

'Fourteen,' I said.

And he said, 'Oh yes, I was away when you came. And how have you found your time with a typical French family?'

Monsieur Blanc's sobs filled the cul-de-sac. I said, 'Errr . . .' and we both laughed. A pause followed. 'I've really liked getting to know Pascale,' I said. 'And Didier, of course, and . . . and you.'

I was pulling the leaves off the plant I was sitting next to and rolling them between my fingers. When I looked up, he was checking his watch. He said, 'I'd better . . . er . . .'

'Where's Didier now?' I said.

'He's gone to talk to our mother. I wanted to go, but he thought he would be better at it.' He stood up.

I stood up too. I was trying not to feel disappointed. I blurted, 'There's a party tomorrow. Are you going to come?'

'A party? Where?'

'At Mimi's. You met her when she spent the night. She lives on the Île de la Cité. It's a fantastic apartment. Her parents are away.'

'Oh, are they?' he said, and then, setting my heart racing again, 'Well, maybe I'll be there.'

💙 *Kitchen, 11.50 a.m.*

Didier is back. I don't think from the setness of his expression that the conversation with his mother went well. I'll have to wait until later to find out because I have to leave RIGHT NOW to meet Mother and Mr Spence.

💙 *RER, between Châtelet-Les Halles and Nation, 4.30 p.m.*

I thought they'd missed the train. I was a little bit late and I got to the Gare du Nord as the Eurostar was pulling in. I ran to the right platform and watched as gaggle after gaggle of weekenders wheeled their suitcases past. A large American woman in turquoise slacks and a baseball cap with 'I've Been To The Planetarium' on it stopped to ask if I could tell her where 'you gotta cab'. I didn't know, but I showed her the picture of a taxi with an arrow above her head and she waddled off. Two teenage girls passed me with their parents. 'Let's do shopping then lunch,' the mother said. 'No, let's do shopping then shopping,' the elder girl said.

No sign of Mother and Mr Spence. The only people still coming off were very old or had masses of luggage, but then, suddenly, behind a couple pushing a trolley laden with suitcases, I saw what I thought was the top of Mother's head, and then to one side of it, a bare hairy leg that looked like it must belong to Mr Spence. And then the couple with the trolley was past the pillar and there they were, behind them, the two of them, coming towards me. Mother, who was in her nicest black suit and her work heels, was beaming from one side of her face to the other, although as she got closer I saw tears were also pouring down her cheeks. Mr Spence, a bag in each hand, stood back while we hugged.

'You're not cross?' I kept saying. 'Promise you're not cross. Or sad? Tell me you're happy.'

She was, she said, still weeping, very happy.

'Your hair!' she said.

'Do you like it?'

'Yes!'

Mr Spence – John – stepped forward and handed her a huge striped handkerchief to wipe her eyes. 'Go on,' he said. 'Have a good blow. You know you want to.'

She blew and then she wiped again. I said, 'Is she OK? Was it all right? She didn't try and run away when you got to Waterloo?'

'No,' she said from behind the handkerchief. 'I didn't.'

'She wanted to see her big girl, didn't you, Bern?'

I said, 'Bern?'

Mother, *always* known as Bernadette, gave me a warning look. 'Let's go and find the hotel.'

Mr Spence insisted we got a taxi. We had to queue. The fat Planetarium woman was way ahead of us, but there were lots of taxis and it didn't take long. Mr Spence read out the address of the hotel in such a terrible French accent, the driver – Algerian, I think – looked blank until Mother took the itinerary from him and read it out herself. 'Best Western Étoile!' she repeated, raising her eyebrows and giving a little squeal of excitement.

Mr Spence looked back at me from the passenger seat and winked.

It was heaven travelling through Paris in a taxi. Mother said, 'I expect this isn't what you've been used to!' and I was about to say, 'No, that's right. The only other time I was in a taxi in Paris I wasn't concentrating on the scenery as I'd been caught shoplifting and just met my grandmother for the first time,' but luckily I stopped myself and told her about the taxi ride through Brussels instead. She said she'd seen the statue of the boy weeing and that it looked nothing like Cyril. She tapped me on the head with her passport and then gave me another big hug.

I wanted to know how everyone was at home. Cyril, a retiring soul who is only happy tucked up on the sofa with a plate of peanut-butter sandwiches watching Pokémon, had been invited to a football party by a boy at school. He'd gone reluctantly, dragging his trainered toes all the way across the playing field, casting reproachful glances over his shoulder at Mother. When she'd returned to pick him up: a changed boy! He had scored three goals, was charging up and down, red, muddy and sweaty, with a gang of other boys and could hardly be dragged away. 'Ah,' Mother and I said in unison, as we flashed past the Gare Saint-Lazare.

She said Marie was her usual bumptious self, had thrown herself to the floor, sobbing and renting her bosom, at the news that Mother was leaving for two days, but had cheered up the moment Jack arrived to take her and C to LEGOLAND. 'Hardly had time to kiss me goodbye,' Mother added.

'And Jack?' I said. 'I hear . . .'

'New girlfriend in telesales.'

'Yes, and . . .'

'New job. Yes. Fruit bowls. Hmm.'

She looked at me and we both laughed. Mother is so over Jack it's not true.

Mr Spence leant over and said, 'I hope you don't laugh at me like that when you've chucked me out.'

Mother began to pout and go coy (she is all kitten as far as men are concerned) so I said, 'She can't chuck you out. You own the house.' And Mother and I fell about laughing again.

'Women,' Mr Spence said. 'Save me from them.'

The Best Western was not as naff as I'd imagined. It was all red and gold carpet and roses in vases. An American family was drinking champagne in the foyer. But the lift creaked and smelt of damp, and there was a mattress leaning against the wall outside their room.

In the bedroom, a fantasy in peach and white, Mother lay down on the bed, bounced up and down a couple of times and rested her head on the pillow. She tapped the mattress next to her and called, 'Chéri!' Mr Spence, who'd just emerged from the bathroom thrilling to the news that the lavatory was hygiene-sealed, went to lie down. I'm still not ready to witness my mother's public displays of affection (with him – yuck) so I made sure I got there first. He had to sit on the stool with thick straps instead of a seat. (What's that about? Is it a special stool especially for luggage? Is that necessary?)

'Now, Constance. Tell me everything. Are you having a lovely, lovely, lovely time?'

It's funny that thing people do: ask you a question with the answer built into it. Mother does it a lot. It's a way of ensuring the world is comfortable around her, a way of keeping the bad out. You can't really reply, 'Um, well, not exactly lovely ...' without sounding churlish. There's no room for disagreement. You either have to agree, or go further in the same direction. As in, not just lovely, FANTASTIC.

'Not just lovely, Mother. FANTASTIC,' I said.

'And is Pascale super, super, super?'

'Um.' I thought for a moment and then laughed to myself. 'Yes,' I said. 'She is. She's very interesting.'

'And Paris, chérie? Is it what you imagined?'

'Yes, Mother,' I said. 'It is. It's – it's lovely.'

'And what have you been doing? Have you been to Sacré Cœur?'

'No. Not Sacré Cœur.'

'Les Tuileries?'

'No, not yet, but . . .'

'Montmartre?'

I shook my head.

'Le Louvre? Le Jeu de Paume?'

'No.'

'The Eiffel Tower? Chérie, Cyril, he is so excited to hear about the Eiffel Tower.'

'No,' I said, surprised. 'I haven't been up the Eiffel Tower. I was going to, but . . .'

'So, Constance. What have you been doing?'

'Well . . .' I couldn't tell her about meeting my grandmother or Pascale's brush with the law. I couldn't tell her that. I couldn't tell her about being kissed by François, or the Crying Girl, or falling in love with Philippe. And, apart from that, what had I been doing?

'I've seen Delilah a few times,' I said. 'That's been nice. And Julie. I've met up with her.'

'Delilah and Julie! You can see them at home!'

'I know.'

'And les Blancs, have they been nice to my little Constance? Are they a good family?'

'Oh, Mother,' I began. Then stopped. I really wanted to tell her about Madame Blanc and her obsessive cleaning and Monsieur Blanc and his bullying and then the crisis of the last few days – the terrible tension, the emotions flying everywhere, the trauma, the embarrassment – but she was looking at me so expectantly and happily, I didn't want to disappoint her.

So, I started making up stories about them. I should have just said, 'They're very nice.' But I said, 'Thérèse – that's Madame Blanc, but she won't let me call her that, in fact the moment I got off the bus, she said, "I'm Thérèse and I'll hear no more about it" – and we wander down to the market together every day. She didn't speak any English when I first arrived, but I've taught her loads. She used to be a ballet dancer and every night, after supper, we all sit round the table and she dances and Monsieur Blanc – Jean – sings. He's got a deep baritone. Didier, that's the elder brother, plays the piano. And Philippe and Pascale and I clap hands and call out, "More, more," until everyone falls to the ground, exhausted.'

'Oh,' said Mother. 'Gosh.'

Mr Spence said, 'Sounds a bit full-on.'

'No, it isn't, it isn't. And then we play Monopoly.'

'In French?' asked Mr Spence.

'Um . . . yeah.'

'So, what's Mayfair?' he laughed.

I thought quickly. 'The Champs Elysées.'

'Of course,' Mother said, smiling.

'And there's this lovely Bohemian aunt who comes to visit and we go for long family walks after church on Sundays, stopping off for bread and cakes –'

'I can see you've been enjoying the cakes.'

'And then we go home and they take it in turns to cook. Sometimes Monsieur Blanc – I mean, Jean – throws steak on the barbecue and Didier and Philippe toss up a salad and –'

'You've had better weather than we have then,' said Mr Spence.

'It's just nice to be part of such a nice, conventional family,' I said.

Mother looked for a moment as if she was going to burst into tears. It's only now, as I sit here on the train, that I think maybe I went too far. But in fact she smiled and said, 'Oh, chérie. I am so glad because staying with a family you do not know could be an unsettling experience. I was worried that it might be so, but I was wrong. It is all wonderful.'

'Yes,' I said. 'It is.'

Mr Spence was standing up by this time, at the double-glazed windows, peering out. He said, 'Bern. Shower. Then hit the town? What do you say?'

'John, I am in your hands.'

She stood up, sighed deeply and then stretched, and

while she was doing so, Mr Spence sidled up and put his arms round her – a bit higher than her waist – as if he was going to lift her off the ground. He isn't that much taller than her when she's got her heels on. Then . . . urgh. 'You're in my hands now,' he said. She smiled into his face. Then he kissed her – not a snog, but longer than necessary, thank you very much.

'Er – hum,' I said. 'Minors present.'

'Sorry.' Mr Spence cleared his throat and stepped back. 'It's just your mother . . . grrrr . . . miaow!'

I made my excuses and left.

Chapter Twenty

New vocab: *un pouf* (a pouffe); *les coussinets de soie*
(silk scatter cushions); *les tea lights* (tea lights)

Still Friday 11 April
❤ *Living room chez les Blancs, 5.30 p.m.*

An atmosphere.

Valérie has rearranged the living-room furniture by
putting the dining table at a different angle and switching
the sofa so that it faces the window rather than the
fireplace. She has brought a pouffe into the house.
Currently she is upstairs in the master bedroom, scat-
tering Moroccan silk cushions. Monsieur Blanc is making
himself a sandwich in the kitchen – I've only seen his
back, but it looks troubled – and the Blanc children are
sulking in the garden.

When I went outside, Pascale said, 'I liked the sofa

❤ 155 ❤

where it was.' And Philippe said, 'I liked the dining table where it was.' And Didier said, 'Maybe she'll have another consignment of Moroccan tea lights to pick up soon.'

'There is no way I am having a pouffe in my bedroom,' added Philippe.

It's odd, but I feel more detached now I've seen Mother, now Mother is in Paris. I'm only going to be with the Blancs until Monday – that's only two and half days. It seemed like I'd be here for ever on Wednesday, but now I'm almost gone. I don't know whether I'm happy or sad.

'I've seen my mother,' I said.

They pretended to be interested but were preoccupied with their own mother. Didier said he had a feeling his mother was *implacable* about the situation. Pascale started crying. She isn't wearing any make-up today so she looks much younger – more my age. 'When is she coming home?' she said. 'She'd hate all the changes Aunt Valérie's making. She wouldn't stand for it.'

Didier and Philippe exchanged glances.

Valérie wafted out, holding a wrought-iron lantern in the shape of an urn in her hand. She was wearing a floaty, white, embroidered kaftan over a pair of linen trousers. Her hair was in a bun. She placed the lantern in the middle of the garden table and stood back a pace. 'There!' she said. 'Much better.'

Nobody said anything.

'Time for church soon,' she said. 'And then home for

a nice fish supper. Pascale, I've put a rather chic bedspread on your bed. It's made by a group of artisans in the Atlas mountains. Brightens up your room a bit, but honestly it is very dark in there. Like the grave.'

Pascale got up and went back into the house.

There was a silence and then Valérie, who was still standing, said, 'Right. I'll go in and get ready. Didier – long trousers for church, please. Philippe – don't forget to wash your hands.'

After she'd gone, Didier said, 'You don't appreciate what you've got until it's gone.'

❤ The garden, 8 p.m.

Back from church.

I'm in the garden on my own. Do you know who I wish I could speak to this minute? William. Just as a friend, of course.

We all lined out of the house to church. I was wearing my new top and trousers, which I'd retrieved from the laundry basket. There was a hot-chocolate stain on the top which I had to dab with some loo roll and the trousers badly needed an iron. I'll have to wash them before the party tomorrow.

When we got to the church door, Philippe whispered something to Valérie and turned as if he were about to escape, but she yanked him by the collar and pushed him into the vestry ahead of her.

It was pretty busy. We sat in a row in a pew near the

back. A stream of people in their best clothes – I recognized the woman from the bakery and Véronique from the driving school – greeted us on their way in. Julie and her family were already sitting on the other side of the church; I managed to catch her eye and we grinned at each other and waved.

Monsieur Blanc sat on the end and spent the whole time craning and half-standing up to see better.

The service began – lots of droning, everyone bowing their heads, crossing themselves, standing, kneeling, counting beads, chanting. We had stood up to sing and had just settled down again when I realized that, behind the pillar, about fifteen rows ahead of us, was the woman from the shoe shop and, next to her, a mac I recognized: Madame Blanc. I nudged Didier, who was sitting next to me and he half-stood to see. Then Monsieur Blanc caught on and had to be restrained by Valérie, who was sitting next to him, from getting up and charging to the front of the church.

During the next hymn, he pulled his jacket from her grasp and slipped into a row two ahead of us. And, as we sat down, he nipped into the row in front of that. I had such an urge to giggle I had to bring the hymn sheet right up close to my face. The priest must have told everyone to pray because the congregation got to its knees – except for Monsieur Blanc, who was continuing to move, surreptitiously, pew by pew, up the church. Then it was time for communion. Most people stood up and started queuing. Monsieur Blanc joined the stream leaving his pew and went straight for the pew where Madame Blanc had been sitting. Valérie tried to make me, but I didn't go up for communion. I stayed where I was. Monsieur Blanc, ten rows ahead, did too. I saw Madame Blanc, leaving the rail, hands clasped. She saw her husband and walked up the church away from him, until she reached my pew, the pew where he'd started off. Then she kneeled down and prayed.

He stood up, but by this time everyone was returning to their seats and by the time he got back to us, the pew was full. Pascale was kneeling by her mother, whispering to her. Philippe and Didier were sitting near them, so Valérie had had to re-enter the pew on the other side, next to me.

Monsieur Blanc stood there, large and bearded, like a supplicant. But then the priest started up again and he squeezed into the pew in front. The woman next to him tutted and waggled her hat like a cross duck.

He bowed his head – he seemed to be writing something. Then, as the priest was giving us his final blessing, he turned and thrust his hymn sheet into his wife's hand.

She didn't look at him, but folded it and put it in her pocket. And then she kissed her children, stood up and disappeared out of the church door.

We all looked for her afterwards, but she'd gone.

Philippe went out to meet some friends after supper. No one had the heart to stop him. I felt low after he'd gone. I thought he might have taken me and Pascale with him, but he didn't offer. Still, he said he'd come to Mimi's party tomorrow. And then I'll have him to myself.

I asked Valérie if I could ring Julie and she said I could, so long as I was quick.

'God, that went on,' Julie said when she came on the line. She's Church of England, which means she never goes to church at home. 'I thought I was going to die of boredom.'

'Think of the sanctity of your soul,' I said.

'It was the aching in my bum I was more worried about.'

I told her about picking up Mother and Mr Spence and she said I was a conniving genius.

'Bit of heavy petting, though,' I said. 'Not so sure about it.'

'Con, she's happy. Give her that.'

She was right. I told her I *was* touched, seeing them together, but also repelled, if that makes sense.

'Sort of,' she said.

❤ *Bathroom, 9 p.m.*

'Darling, I haven't seen you for AGES. This week has been, like, mad.'

It was Delilah on the phone. Only it didn't sound like Delilah. It sounded like Mimi.

'We've been, like, having the most wonderful time – *formidable*. That means "wonderful" in French –'

'I know,' I said.

'Carol and Bob – Mimi's parents – they are très, très cool. Nice was just . . . *formidable.* Mimi's friend Sacha from Benenden is here – she's, like, well cool. We've only got Eva, their Filipino housekeeper, to look after us and she's, like, a pushover. Mimi's slipped her 100 euros and she's made herself scarce. Now we are seeing you tomorrow, aren't we, babe? Can't wait.'

'Delilah?' I said. 'This is me, Constance. Your next-door neighbour. You can talk normally if you like.'

'Hel-lo? I *am* talking normally.'

'No, you're not. You're like a chameleon. You talk all Estuary when you're with me or William. Now you're talking like a trust-fund princess.'

'Am not.'

'Are so. But anyway, yes, I am coming. Pascale and her brother are coming too if that's all right.'

'*Super.*' She said this with a French accent. 'Listen, you couldn't do me a favour, could you? You couldn't ring William for me? I'm trying to get him to come over – I really want to show him off. Mimi doesn't believe he exists, and he's been all down in the mouth, stick in the mud if you know what I mean. Won't come. But if you rang and pleaded he might.'

'Why would me pleading make a difference?' I tried not to sound pleased.

'It's just you could tell him how much I'm missing him, how I'm moping about without him . . . objective witness and all.'

I told her I might, but only if she stopped the Mimi act. She told me to go over there early tomorrow to get changed.

❤ *P's bedroom, 9.30 p.m.*

Felt nervous ringing William. I wouldn't have done it just to please Delilah, but I did so feel like talking to him.

He was his same old self – a bit gruff at first as if he had a mouth full of marbles. He rang me back to save on the Blancs' bill (I was getting dirty looks from Valérie) and by then he'd taken the phone upstairs. His dad had had the day off work and had been in the pub since lunchtime. There seemed to be a fight going on with his mum downstairs – I could hear swearing and crashing until William slammed his bedroom door shut on them.

'My brother said I can go and live with him and his girlfriend next year,' he said.

'Maybe that would be good,' I said.

William breaks my heart sometimes. Here I am in Paris, mooning after Philippe and worrying about the expansion of my hips, and William's back where he always is, dealing with all that.

'I have a proposition,' I said. 'Come to Paris tomorrow. Come to Mimi's party. It's twenty-nine quid on the coach.'

'Nah,' he said.

'William, please.'

'Why should I?'

'Because you owe it to the Paris youth to show them the length and width of your jeans. They all wear slightly too short drainpipes here. You need to introduce them to a whole new world of trousers.'

He laughed, but didn't say anything.

'Go on. Please come. I promised Delilah I'd get you to.'

'Oh, that's it, is it? You're doing Delilah's business. I know she wants me to come because she's been texting me all week.'

'I want you to come,' I said and I meant it.

But it didn't cut any ice.

Chapter Twenty-one

New vocab: *un bronzage artificiel* (a fake tan)

Saturday 12 April
♥ *RER, 11 a.m.*

Major developments:

1. Monsieur Blanc has discovered that Madame Blanc is living with Michel from l'*auto-école*. He went to get the baguettes this morning and the woman behind the counter told him everything as she was handing him his change. He went straight there. The driving school was closed and, though he leant on the bell of the flat above the shoe shop for fifteen minutes, nobody came down to let him in. He's in a heap in the garden now, with Valérie in attendance.

2. Pascale has finished with Eric. He turned up this morning, revving his engine in the street. He wanted them both to go off somewhere for the day, but she told him she couldn't leave her father and he said, 'Make a choice,' and she did. Afterwards she cried for half an hour in the kitchen. Valérie, who had just nailed a decorative leatherwork frieze to the wall above the oven and was in the process of rearranging the cutlery drawer, told her Eric wasn't good enough for her anyway. She'd never liked him much. Pascale stormed upstairs, screaming, 'Who do you think you are? You're not my mum!'

3. Didier has written to his mother detailing the changes Valérie has made to the house. He has described the leatherwork frieze in some detail.

I've left all this behind, though. I'm off to Paris to meet Delilah, Mimi and a friend of hers called Sacha, and then get ready for the party. It's strange to think of Mother being a few miles away and yet not seeing her today, though I'll see them both tomorrow. I hope she and Mr Spence are having fun. I wonder what they're doing. Oh, God, I wish I hadn't let myself wonder that.

I've brought my new – but not that clean – clothes in a carrier bag, and my PJs because I'm staying the night. I wish I could have thought of a way to make Pascale promise not to steal anything. I'm sure she won't.

I think it was just a phase. She's spending the afternoon with her father and coming up with her brothers later.

Note I said, 'brothers'. I sat next to Didier while he was writing to his mother and afterwards he turned to me and said, 'This party tonight. Philippe and Pascale are coming. May I come too?'

I went really red. It's awful that I hadn't thought to invite him. I muttered something about how I'd assumed it wasn't his bag, but of course he was welcome.

I feel in my bones tonight is going to be MOMEN-TOUS. Philippe is going to forget the domestic turmoil that has worried him so this week. He is going to see me for the fourteen-year-old girl I am rather than his little sister's little friend. Delilah says she'll lend me make-up. I've got the killer clothes from last weekend. I know he's been cool all week, but he's had a lot on his mind. I have hope. I keep remembering that look he gave me when I rubbed his ankle in the street. It's got to mean something. Hasn't it?

Here's Châtelet-Les Halles. Wish me luck.

❤ *Mimi's bedroom, 3 p.m.*

Hilarious afternoon so far. Quick update before the evening – or rather, la soirée de Mimi – begins.

Mimi and Sacha, her friend 'from Benenden', were out when I got to the apartment. Delilah had the place to herself and was celebrating by listening to some music very loud. It was some old CD of Mimi's dad called Santana and the song was called 'She's Not There'. We got overexcited and started jumping all over the room during the chorus, screaming, 'She's not there!' at the top of our voices. Then we looked through the photo albums which were all beautiful pale pink or aquamarine suede (tried not to get them mucky with our fingers). In one book there were photographs of Mimi as a baby, tightly curled in a Moses basket, or in a spotty bikini under a sunshade on a sun-kissed beach. In later books, she and her thin, tanned mother (who looks like Mimi with extra lines) are posing by a sparkling turquoise pool, or in skiing gear against a snowbound mountain. 'That's the life of an only child for you,' I said.

'It's not what my life's like,' Delilah replied crossly.

'Not far off.'

'Just because you're an only doesn't mean you're spoilt. And anyway, Mimi's dad is miles richer than Daddy.'

'How can you tell?'

'You just can. He's less, I don't know, *stressed*.'

I had told her about my conversation with William, but she hadn't seemed as fed up as I'd thought. She'd said, 'Tosser,' but affectionately.

Now I surveyed the apartment in all its whiteness. 'God, Del, do you think the party's going to be OK? Do you remember the mess after yours?'

'It'll be fine,' she said. 'Julie's going to sleep over too, so there're lots of us to help clear up.'

'Oh, is she?' I said, suppressing a deeply unattractive spasm of jealousy.

Mimi and Sacha got back before I could worry any more. They had been out to buy wine, beer and olives and stuff – what Mother calls 'bits'.

'Yummy, nibbles,' Delilah said as they unpacked them in the kitchen.

Sacha looked at her over her shoulder. 'Crudités, babe,' she corrected.

Sacha is tall and long-limbed, with defiantly streaked black and blonde hair. She has a stud in her tongue and holes in the knees of her jeans. When she took off her sunglasses, her eyes were the most surprising petrol blue. (Coloured contacts, according to D.) She says, 'Yeah, cool,' all the time, and 'Yeah, chill, chill.'

She looked at me for the first hour or so as if I was something she'd got stuck to the bottom of her shoes. But I wore her down with my friendliness (I was tempted to be snooty too, but decided life was too long). I asked her lots of questions about herself: people always like that. Mimi, who was wearing a pretty sundress and cowboy boots, is being much friendlier than the last time we were here. She has to be nice to me because she's spent a night on my floor.

It's turned into summer since last weekend. The other three girls already had light tans from their few days in the south. Along with the crudités, Mimi had bought some fake tan in a bottle. She had also bought a loofah and a tub of coconut exfoliant to rub off everyone's dead skin cells.

Mother's always saying that the problem with cosmetic surgery is, if you're the only person who hasn't had Botox or a face lift you look like an old crone in comparison. The same law applies to fake tan. By the time Mimi, Sacha and Delilah had sanded and anointed and were down to their pants – sitting, arms and legs apart on towels – in Delilah's bedroom, I had begun to look like a slab of whale blubber.

'I'm fine,' I said when Sacha started badgering me. 'Pale but intéressante.'

'You're certainly pale,' she said.

We were all the best of friends by then and started rolling around laughing.

'Don't. Don't,' squeaked Mimi, 'I'll smudge.'

Then she farted – it was hysterical coming from her, uptight as she is – and we really started laughing then. You know the sort of laughter when it hurts?

'What a smudge!' Delilah said. 'Poo-ey.'

And that set us off again.

So . . . I'm tanned too now. I'm sitting drying in my knickers with the others. And it's quite good. The only drawbacks are streaky knees and ankles, and hands that look as if we've rubbed them in nicotine. Oh, and I smell like a diesel engine. Apart from that: très sexy.

(Quick aside. Can you tell a person's personality from their choice of pants? If so:

Mimi

A tiny white thong, decorated along the top with expensive-looking pink daisies. 'What pretty knickers,' I said. And she said, 'Broderie anglaise.' I've looked it up in the dictionary. It basically means lace. English lace. But in French. That seems to sum Mimi up. Pretty, girly, neat and involved in some slight Anglo/Franco confusion.

Sacha

A pair of snug boy's-style white boxer shorts, low slung, with 'Girl Boxer' (or possibly 'Boxer Girl') written eight times along the waistband (though it's more of a hipband). Like their owner: trendy, fit, sexy in an I-don't-care way.

Delilah

Oh, Delilah. Her knickers are bikini-style, black lace and diaphanous. They do up with bows at the side. Embroidered in red at the front is a cartoon-style cat with a big grin. That's my girl. Never afraid to be too obvious. Half sex kitten, half Disney.

Clearly I am not going to include myself in this list as my PANTS – M&S finest, once white, now grey, possibly slightly on the over-large size – have already been the cause of much hilarity. Delilah told the others that my mother worked for a posh underwear shop – By Appointment to the Queen, I added – and that made them giggle all the more. I don't care. I like making people laugh. And I like being comfortable. And anyway, even if I do get off with Philippe tonight, he's not going to get that close to notice. End of aside.)

The beauty salon continues. The others say I'm not allowed to write in here any more. We are to become ladies.

❤ *Mimi's bedroom, 7 p.m.*

Mimi is in the kitchen scoffing her fourth pancake – 'Crêpe, babe' – with chocolate spread. Sacha is smoking on the balcony. Delilah and I are in the bedroom having a competition to see who can make the loudest burps.

Just thought I'd keep you updated.

Chapter Twenty-two

New vocab: *pris en flagrant délit* (caught in the act)

Sunday 13 April
♥ *Mimi's kitchen, 1 a.m.*

It's funny how sometimes you worry about the wrong things. I was so anxious about Mimi's apartment. I thought there would be cigarette burns on the floorboards. I didn't think about my fingers being burnt. I was worried about Pascale coming in and nicking stuff. I didn't think Delilah would do the same.

We were all getting on well at the beginning of the evening, Mimi, Sacha, Delilah and me. I know we're all different, but it didn't seem to matter. Mimi's fart was the beginning of the end as far as being sensible was concerned. We giggled and mucked about so much it was almost 8 p.m. when we got round to getting dressed.

This, for me, was a sobering experience. Putting on my brown trousers and plum long-sleeved T-shirt didn't take long, so I sat on Mimi's bed and watched while the others finished. Mimi was wearing a red dress that wrapped around her, with a pair of round-toed high-heeled shoes. Sacha wore her jeans with a tight, apple-green cashmere cardigan and nothing but a pink bra underneath. You could see a lot of bra and a lot of flat brown tummy. Delilah took a long time choosing, but plumped finally for a tiny white skirt, a thick black belt slung across her hips and a sequinned halter-neck top. She brushed her thick brown hair until it was as shiny as the mane on a chestnut pony. Sometimes she slaps on too much make-up but this evening she was just wearing red lipstick. She looked gorge – they all did.

'You all look amazing,' I said mournfully from the bed.

'You do too,' said Sacha unconvincingly.

It was only a week since I felt like the belle of the ball, but it all went wrong tonight. The brown trousers felt baggy and a bit grubby – Madame Blanc not being around meant they didn't get washed. And the plum top looked and felt dull. The problem was the sun – I was wintry, everyone else was summery. My short hair had lost its newness, too, and it dried in an odd, sticky-up way. I felt gangly and flat next to the three others in their bright spangly colours. Even my tan felt, well, just brown.

Looking back, I wonder if the problem was because

I felt dull, rather than that I *was* dull. Maybe beauty isn't in the eye of the beholder but in the power of the giver. Delilah never doubts herself. She may not be the slimmest cracker on the cheeseboard, but it doesn't dent her confidence. She thinks she's beautiful and so she is. I suppose there's a lesson in there somewhere.

Anyway, the others couldn't have been sweeter. Sacha even tried to lend me some strappy heels, but we all decided I looked like a transvestite in them so I took them off.

We put some music on, poured ourselves a drink and waited.

The first people to arrive were Thomas and Anne, a couple, who both looked about eighteen. Thomas was the son of some friends of Mimi's parents. They went round kissing everybody on each cheek and then sat on the sofa holding hands and making polite conversation with Mimi, who perched on the edge of the coffee table.

The next person to arrive was an older boy called Dave, who was wearing shorts, flip-flops and a bemused expression. He had long, thick brown hair, full of split ends, that looked like he might keep bees in it. It took me a while to place his accent. When I said, 'Where are you from?' he answered, 'I am a citizen of the world,' though he later admitted he was from New Zealand. He's been travelling since the March before last.

I said, 'How do you know Mimi?'

'I don't,' he said.

It turns out she and Sacha had got talking to him when they'd been out shopping this morning and they'd invited him along.

It got to 9 p.m. and no one else had turned up.

I said to Delilah, when I got her on her own, 'Who's coming?'

'You know, people.'

'But who?'

'Well ...' She looked shifty. 'Mimi is at school in England. She doesn't have *many* friends here ...'

'Does she have any?'

'Er ...' She didn't get to answer, because Thomas and Anne came out to kiss us both goodbye.

'So, then there were three,' I said.

'And Dave. Don't forget Dave.'

We both laughed.

We were on the balcony at this point. It was cool and dark, but you could still feel the warmth from the day in the bricks behind you. If you leant back, you could see birds still wheeling high in the sky above. You could hear the distant rumble of traffic. You could smell the river.

'How's your week been?'

I looked at Delilah in surprise. 'Oh,' I said.

'Has it been OK living with Pascale? Have you had a nice time?'

It was such a rare honour to be asked a question by Delilah, I couldn't think of anything to say.

'How about those delicious brothers of hers?'

'Funny you should say that . . .' I began, 'because I really like Philippe and –'

I was about to confide in her, to tell her about last week's kiss and my hopes for tonight, but there were noises and voices in the apartment then. Lots of people had arrived all at once.

We went back into the living room. Julie was there, in a funky dress over jeans. She was wearing bright red lipstick and a big smile. 'You are so BROWN!' she was shrieking at all of us. 'I'm so CROSS. I'd have had a sunbed if I'd known. Con!' She saw me. 'You too!'

'I'm sorry,' I said. 'I've let you down.'

Coming into the room behind her were Pascale, Didier and Philippe. All three looked subdued and embarrassed. Mimi was getting them drinks. Pascale was very pale. (Particularly when she stood next to Mimi.)

'People!' I said. 'At last!'

Philippe grinned. 'Where's the party?' he said.

'Out there.' I gestured to the balcony, where Dave and Sacha were talking.

'Crudités, anyone?' Delilah appeared with a plate of olives.

Philippe pretended to scoop the whole lot up. Delilah pretended to spank his bottom.

Julie pulled me into the corner. 'I've got to ask you. Tomorrow! Lunch. Are you all set up?'

'Lunch? Tomorrow?' Delilah and Philippe were still mucking about with the olives. She was trying to put stones down the back of his shirt. He had hold of her arm and she was squealing.

'Your mother? Your grandparents? Get with it. You know, the reunion of the century?'

'Oh, that. Yes. Of course.'

'I was wondering, are your grandparents going to be at the table when she comes in or will they arrive after she's sat down?'

'Julie, er . . . what do you think?'

Philippe and Delilah had gone out on to the balcony.

'Tricky. Personally I think it might be better if she was sitting down when they turned up . . . Connie, what's the matter?'

'Oh. I'm just . . . Nothing.'

'What does your grandmother think?'

'About what?'

'About who should get there first. You're not concentrating, are you?'

'Julie, it's just . . . Do you think I've got a chance with Philippe?'

She followed my eyes. 'Oh.' She is such a good friend. She understood at once. 'Yes I do. But not if Delilah gets there first. Go!'

On the balcony, Sacha and Dave were smoking and discussing world politics. Delilah and Philippe were discussing Delilah. 'I come from quite a deprived background,' Delilah was saying. There was lipstick on the rim of her glass.

Philippe smiled warmly when he saw me. 'My little

English girl,' he said (hope!) and put his arm round my shoulder (double hope!!). I tried not to stiffen. I tried to breathe normally.

Delilah began telling us about the ballet classes she used to have when she was little. Her arms were raised, showing off her port de bras. 'First position. Second position. Third and fourth. And fifth position,' she was chanting, displaying her body in an array of beguiling positions. Philippe was laughing.

I launched into a description of the fake-tanning process, complete with naked girls in knickers. I told Philippe my Theory of Pants and he thought that was very funny. Delilah, who had heard it already, thought it was funny too. She took off her shoes and started inspecting the inside of her toes. 'Look, white bits!' she said to me. She was leaning on Philippe for balance. From where I was standing you could see her inner thighs, which weren't white at all.

Who knows which of us would have given in first. But Mimi stuck her head through the door and made us all come into the living room. She put us in teams and organized a game of charades. I was with Pascale, Didier and Julie. My *Bonjour Tristesse* (a seminal book by Françoise Sagan, according to Mimi) won the day. Didier got my wave and handshake (the '*Bonjour*' bit) immediately. Philippe, Delilah, Dave, Sacha and Mimi struggled gamely with *Macbeth*. Delilah did her best to act the whole thing – lots of stabbing and washing of hands – but they gave in. We were all laughing so much it didn't matter.

After that, Sacha chose more music and she and Dave danced madly around the apartment. Mimi and Didier joined in, more sedately. The rest of us lounged about. I lounged next to Philippe. My leg touched his. We all drank quite a lot and I felt as if I was in a movie. Time didn't seem to matter. The evening was stretching like elastic.

And then I realized Pascale, who was curled up like a black cat on a chair opposite and who had been very quiet all evening, was crying.

I got up and went to her. 'What's the matter?' I said, putting my arm round her. 'What's up? Is it your mother?'

'No.'

'Is it Eric?'

She didn't answer.

I held her for a while, and then I got her a drink of water. 'Do you want to talk about it?'

She nodded and we went through to Mimi's bedroom and sat on the bed.

It took a while before she could talk. 'It's everything,' she said. 'Maman and . . . Eric. I wish he was here. I don't know if I love him, but I miss him now. It's been such a horrible week.'

I immediately felt guilty. I haven't been very thoughtful, have I?

'Poor you,' I said. 'It's all so traumatic. But your parents love you, you know that, don't you?'

She was twisting Mimi's nightdress – a little lacy number – in her fingers. 'It's my fault,' she was sobbing.

'No it's not.'

'It is. I've been so bad. And they argue about me.'

'It's not what it's about. I'm sure. In my book, *Madame Bovary* ...' I tried to tell her about Emma Bovary's yearning for something else beyond the domestic sphere. Pascale was looking at me oddly and after a few minutes I realized literature isn't always helpful.

'Is there anything I can do?' I said.

'I want to go home.'

'Shall I get Didier?'

'No, Philippe. Can you get Philippe?'

So, I left the bedroom and went back into the living room. Philippe wasn't there, so I went out on to the balcony.

I don't want to remember it. I don't want to remember the way they were sitting side by side, like the star sign for Gemini. I don't want to remember the way his eyes were closed, or the way she was running her pretty, plump hands through his hair.

I stepped back into the living room. I could hear Mimi, Didier and Julie's voices in the kitchen. Sacha and Dave were on the sofa, playing backgammon with a beautiful handmade set that had sat on the shelf in the alcove. There was a space there now, and, with my back to them, I ran my fingers across the dust round the square where it had been. I picked up one of the photo albums Delilah and I had looked at earlier and opened it at random. I stared at a picture of Mimi and her immaculate mother drinking coffee in an Italian square. Some people have life on a plate. I remembered Delilah's grumpiness earlier, her beef that Mimi's parents are richer than hers, that Mimi has 'a better deal' than she does. It struck me it wouldn't occur to me to be jealous, to launch some invidious chain of comparisons, because I'm not in the same league as either of them.

This trip to Paris was my adventure. The only adventure I'd ever had. And Delilah had hijacked it. I know it wasn't her fault she'd taken William away from me. I hadn't told her how I felt about him. It wasn't her fault she'd taken Philippe away from me either. I hadn't told her about last week's kiss. But why hadn't I? Do I keep things from her because I'm scared she's going to take them away from me? Then I had a worse thought. Had she guessed both times? Is that why she'd taken both of them?

She's a magpie. If it glistens, she has to have it. But do things only glisten because she sees them through my eyes?

A big wet tear dropped on to the aquamarine suede photo album. I watched it widen into a stain. Then I pulled myself together. Self-pity is not an attractive quality.

I went into the kitchen. Julie was telling a story about some antic of Virginie's little sister. Didier looked at me, with his head on one side; a kind dog with soft brown eyes.

'*Ça va?*' he asked.

'Yes,' I said. I wanted to go home badly. Really home – all the way to London. Homesickness and disappointment and self-contempt swirled together like a great vat of muesli in my stomach. 'But Pascale needs you. She's in the bedroom.'

'Oh.' We went through together and I stood in the doorway while he talked to her. She said she wanted Eric to come and get her and Didier rang him from his mobile phone. 'He's coming,' he said when he'd hung up. 'I couldn't have stopped him if I'd tried.'

Pascale giggled through her tears. She wanted to stay in Mimi's bedroom until he got there. She wanted some time alone. Didier got up and left. I stood and looked at her for a few minutes.

I said, 'You can put that back under the pillow where you found it.'

'What?'

'That nightie. Put it back.'

Sheepishly, she pulled Mimi's lacy thing out of her sleeve.

'I'm watching you,' I said.

At least she was feeling more herself.

I followed Didier back into the kitchen.

'Oh, Didier!' Mimi had her head in the fridge. 'We've run out of ice. Will you be a honey and nip out and get some?'

(I've written this, as per, in English, but I think it's important for posterity to acknowledge that she spoke to him, as per, in French.)

'But of course,' Didier replied. He turned to me and said, in careful English, 'Would you like some fresh air, Constance?'

There was nothing I wanted more, so I found my coat and, ignoring Julie's troubled look, followed him out.

'You're a bit quiet,' he said as we descended the stairs. 'Not enjoying the party?'

'Yes.'

'Though it's not much of a party.'

'No.'

We'd reached the street. I looked up and he followed my eyes. You could just make out Delilah and Philippe making out on the balcony.

Didier frowned. 'Oh,' he said.

I tried to laugh, but it came out wrong. 'Everyone loves Philippe,' I said. 'Isn't that what you all say?' I hadn't meant to sound bitter.

'Oh, Constance. Has my silly little brother taken your heart?'

'No,' I said. Didier looked at me. 'Yes,' I said.

We walked across the bridge in silence. The Seine smelt dank and green, of sand and silt and tortoises. We took a narrow road up towards the Marais. The air felt warm, with a cool breeze coming up from the river. After a while I felt Didier's arm round my shoulder. It was awkward. My step was out of sync and I had to do a half-skip every few paces to keep up. We passed some stores selling kebabs with lots of people milling outside.

Didier went into one of them and came out with a bag of ice cubes. We set off back in the direction we'd come, towards Mimi's apartment.

'Oh. There's the *Hôtel de Ville*,' I said. 'It looks lovely. I really wanted my mother to stay there but it's too posh.'

Didier laughed. 'It's not a hotel,' he said. 'It's the town hall. Has no one explained that?'

'No.'

'Or pointed out the sights?'

'Not really.'

'Let me show you some places. They won't miss us.'

Didier led me down to the Rue de Rivoli to the Musée de Louvre, where he pointed out the glass pyramid entrance. We walked on and he told me about Napoleon building the Arc de Triomphe in homage to himself and his army. At the Place de la Concorde, we crossed the river and walked back. Paris felt grand and imperious. Traffic passed us at speed. After a while, he took my hand.

We must have been gone an hour. When we reached the Pont Neuf, we sat on a bench and Didier talked about his worries about his mother – how glad he was that she had escaped from his father, but how anxious he was about Pascale. I told him my plans for my mother and grandparents. A cold breeze swept across the river and I shivered. He put his arm round me. I leant into him. I wondered what was happening back at the apartment, whether the others were worried about us. I felt bad about Julie – unless new people had arrived she wasn't going to be having the most wonderful of times. She's used to parties being, well, parties. I wondered whether the game of backgammon had finished, whether anyone had reloaded the CD player, whether Philippe and Delilah . . .

'We'd better go back,' I said. 'They'll be wondering what's happened to us.'

Didier stood up reluctantly and we continued across the bridge, on to the island, and into Mimi's street.

I was ahead of him and he stopped behind me, still holding on to my hand. 'Constance!' He sounded urgent.

I turned.

'May I kiss you?' he asked.

Could I kiss a second Blanc brother? Wasn't that some complicated form of incest? Did I want to? Could I feel something for him? If I did, would I feel better about myself or worse? And then I thought: who cares?

So, I leant towards him.

Our lips were a second away from meeting when I saw someone walking towards us, someone achingly familiar. My heart leapt.

I pulled my hand out of Didier's grasp, turned and ran towards him.

'William!'

'Yup. That's me,' William said. 'Constance, you're crushing me.'

I let him go. His hair was all over the place. He had

a tatty rucksack over his shoulder, his parka was open, and his jeans were hanging down around his hipbones.

'What are you doing here!'

'You invited me.'

'But you came!'

'I thought you wanted me to.'

'I did. I do. I'm . . .'

'You missed me, you said.'

'I did!'

'What have you done with your hair? What are you *wearing*?' William looked me up and down with a slight frown on his face.

'Hello.' Didier, all pressed and neat, was standing next to us, with his hand out. 'I am Didier.'

William shook it. 'Hi. I'm William.' He looked from Didier to me and then back to Didier again. 'Hello,' he said. 'So . . .'

'So.' I was grinning. I had to resist the temptation to throw my arms round him again. 'It's almost midnight,' I said.

'I know. I've been walking for ages. I didn't realize it was so far. And then I forgot the apartment number. I thought I'd be able to find it because of the noise, but . . .'

'It's just up here,' I said, pulling him towards Mimi's door.

We rang the doorbell, the door buzzed and the three of us went up the stairs. I wanted William to myself, but I also wanted to show him off. I didn't remember Delilah until we were almost at the door. Over my shoulder, I said cheerfully, 'Delilah's going to –' and I was about to say 'wet her pants'. And then I stopped. 'William,' I said. 'Stay exactly where you are.'

Still Sunday
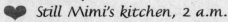 *Still Mimi's kitchen, 2 a.m.*

It's funny how many things you can fit into a split second. The second I remembered about Delilah's latest conquest was the same split second that the idea flashed through my head that William seeing Delilah kissing someone else was the ideal way to separate them, to pave the way for me, his true love. But it was in the same split second I discarded the idea. I love William and I don't want to hurt him, and Delilah, for all that she exasperates the living daylights out of me, is a friend and I couldn't do it to her.

Is it at moments like this that one's mettle is tested? (Or is it metal? If it is, I know I'm not gold, but I might be copper. Aluminium at least.)

'Stay there,' I said. 'Don't move an inch.'

'What about me?' said Didier.

William said, 'Can't I surprise her? I've come all this way.'

'No,' I said. 'Trust me. Just wait.'

I went up the rest of the stairs and into the apartment,

shutting the door behind me. Mimi, Sacha, Julie and Dave were lying on the floor, talking and throwing olive stones into the wastepaper basket. Jazz piano was coming from the CD. No sign of D or P.

'Where are Delilah and Philippe?' I asked.

'Connie!' Julie was the only one to look up. 'Where've you been?'

'I'm looking for Delilah,' I said. 'Where is she?'

She shrugged and I marched across to the balcony (a little bit of me, just a tiny bit of me, was enjoying the crisis, the power, the intrigue) and threw open the doors. They weren't there.

William or Didier had begun knocking on the door to the apartment.

'Er,' Julie said. 'Er . . .' She nudged the others. Mimi looked at me oddly. 'The, er, maybe . . . ?' She gestured towards her bedroom.

'Connie!' William was calling me. 'Let us in.'

'Wait a second!' I said. Delilah and Philippe weren't in the bedroom. I looked in the kitchen. And the bathroom. They weren't there either. Maybe they'd gone out for a romantic walk.

'Let us in, please.'

Julie opened the door before I could stop her.

The two boys trooped in. 'The boy William,' Julie said. 'What the hell?'

He shuffled his feet and looked down at the floor. 'Yeah,' he answered. 'Yeah, well, yeah.'

That's what I love about him: he's so articulate.

She turned to me and made a face that conveyed understanding combined with relief. Before she saw William she must have thought that I'd been on a jealous mission. 'Ahh,' she said, turning. 'Mimi, this is Delilah's boyfriend.'

'Ahh,' said Mimi.

Some embarrassed introductions were made. William looked suddenly racked with the awkwardness of his position. Technically he was gatecrashing. He'd spent however many pounds, travelled however many miles (more attention needed in Geog), walked for hours to gatecrash a party that didn't seem to exist, thrown partly by his girlfriend, who seemed to have left.

'Del. She around?' he asked after a few moments.

'Yes,' Mimi said. 'Yes. Thing is: where? Have you checked . . .' She gestured again towards her bedroom.

'Yes,' I said. 'Yes. Yes I have.'

'Let's get you a drink.' Julie pulled him by the arm into the kitchen.

'They were here,' hissed Mimi after they'd gone. 'A few minutes ago, I'm sure. They only came in from the balcony because Delilah was cold. She was wearing Philippe's jumper. This is awful. *Une catastrophe*.'

'I know,' I said.

'Poor boy,' said Sacha, from the floor.

William and Julie walked back in.

'Bummer,' added Dave with authority.

Where was she? What had she done with herself, the little minx?

We tried to smooth it over, sitting him down on the sofa, changing the music, asking him questions about his journey. After a while I realized he was still wearing his parka so I made him take it off and hang it on the hook by the door. Sacha decided she knew him from somewhere. 'Are you in a band?' she said. 'Are you sure? Didn't you play at the Benenden Christmas dance?'

I couldn't relax. I was listening out for footsteps on the stairs, for a giveaway giggle.

Mimi sidled over to me. 'Did you check my parents' room?' she whispered.

'No!' The very thought.

'Go,' she hissed.

Why would Delilah use Mimi's parents' room? Why, when she had the whole apartment to choose from? It wasn't exactly Piccadilly Circus around here. Surely she wouldn't have.

She had.

They were lying on the bed, rumpled but fully clothed and, like Sleeping Beauty and Prince Charming, fast asleep.

I shook her awake. 'Delilah! William's here. Get up and get out there.'

She half sat and looked at me, dazed. 'I'm not asleep,' she said. (People hate admitting to being asleep.) 'Just resting.'

'Del. William is here.' I had to shout-whisper it to get her to understand.

'William?'

'Yes.'

'What about him?'

'He's here.'

'Here?'

'Yes. Now. Get up. Look surprised. Come on!'

She got off the bed, still half asleep, and slipped on her shoes. Philippe slept on, his mouth half open, a tiny swirl of saliva dribbling from it.

I drew Delilah by the arm into the sitting room, producing her like a prize – a dazed salmon I'd caught in the upper reaches of the Seine.

'Here she is!'

'William.' She looked stunned. 'You came!' She stumbled over to him and threw herself into his lap. He gave me a startled look over her shoulder.

Everyone gave a collective sigh of relief and started drifting off. Crisis averted.

William said, 'Party of the century, eh? Good thing I came to liven it up.' And Delilah decided to quieten him down by snogging him. I felt a pain somewhere in my heart.

Alone in the kitchen, I made myself a cup of tea. The teabags have strings in France and I dipped it up and down over the cup. Up and down. Watching the drips. It's not often you lose two boys to the same girl in one night.

Julie came in and put her arm round my shoulder and watched the teabag with me. 'Bummer,' she said in a New Zealand accent.

I didn't quite have it in me to answer.

Then Didier was in the room too. He stood in the door stiffly. 'I've come to say goodbye.'

'Oh, God! Pascale!' I'd forgotten about her *again*.

Julie said, 'Eric came and picked her up on his bike.'

'I'll check she has got home safely,' said Didier.

He's a nice boy, grown-up and serious and kind, but I didn't want to kiss him. I would have only been making do. You can't go around kissing everybody just because they ask you.

'What about Philippe?' I said.

'He can look after himself.' Didier shrugged. 'He usually does.'

Suddenly, we heard a squeal from the living room. We rushed in to find Philippe on top of Delilah. She was pushing him off. 'No. No! My boyfriend's here. He got here when you were asleep. Philippe! Stop!'

There was a slight noise behind us. William was standing in the doorway, on his way back from the loo.

He just looked at her. He had this expression on his face. I'd seen it before: that day when I walked home from school with him after he'd made the first team in football and his mum and dad had said they'd turn up to watch and they hadn't. We stood outside his house then. You could hear them shouting at each other from the pavement. He stood there then with the same look on his face. I suppose you'd call it disappointment, except that it's rawer than that. It's as if, for a moment, you see everything: everything that all the stuff that's normally in his face – the grins and the grimaces and the posturing – keeps out.

He said, 'Oh, Del,' but lightly, in the tone of voice he'd use if he discovered she'd taped over *Match of the Day*.

'Will.' She came over and stood by him. 'It's nothing. It was just a quick . . . I didn't know you were coming, remember.'

Over on the sofa, Philippe was laughing. 'Oh no. I am found out,' he was saying loudly – in English – to the others. 'The jealous boyfriend has come in.'

Except William . . . well . . . he wasn't being like that. He was smiling oddly.

'William. Please forgive me. I'm so sorry. I've had too much to drink. I –'

'It's OK.'

She was trying to kiss him and he was gently pulling away.

'Why won't you kiss me then?'

He gave her a kiss and she put her arms round him. 'Say it's OK. Say you forgive me.'

'It's OK. I forgive you.'

I left the room then. It was too painful, for all sorts of reasons, to watch. Sometimes I wonder whether I love William in the way a mother loves a child. I know he's fit – well, he is these days. It's funny I never noticed it before – but I also want to protect him. I can't bear seeing him hurt.

Julie joined me back in the kitchen and we sat down at the table. She said she thought William was a saint. She also said she didn't think he was in love with Delilah, he just hoped he was and that it was a different thing.

I said, 'Why isn't he in love with me?'

And she said, 'Maybe he is, but he hopes he isn't.'

'But why?' I said. 'Why make it so complicated?'

'Because you're his friend. He won't want to lose you. He might be scared you'll go off him. And then he'd lose you as a friend as well. Relationships, Constance, *are* complicated.'

She only calls me Constance when she's being really, really serious. It was nice talking to her properly again. That's the problem with being in France. I feel so dislocated from everyone. I know I've seen her loads, but there have always been other people around and it's as if she's a different person here. Maybe I am too. And Delilah's been around so much.

'I don't like you being friends with Delilah,' I said as we sat there. 'It makes me feel left out.'

She laughed. 'Why?'

'I feel like you must talk about me behind my back.'

'We don't.'

'Well, like you might like her more than me.'

'Of course I don't, you pill.'

I felt a whole weight leave my shoulders then.

She said, 'You know something, you and William, you've got to talk. You've got to thrash this one out. You've got to talk it through.'

She went to bed shortly after that and I stayed in the kitchen to write in here. It's really, really late (or early, depending on your viewpoint).

I've just poked my head into the living room. William and Delilah are asleep on the sofa. Dave and Sacha are curled up together on some cushions (that one happened without me noticing). In Mimi's parents' bedroom Mimi and Philippe (that happened without me noticing) are asleep on the floor. Julie's in Mimi's bed and I'm about to budge her up to make room for me.

Chapter Twenty-three

New vocab: er, too busy for that . . .

❤ *Mimi's bedroom, 5 a.m.*

I was destined to have no sleep. And I don't care. I've got the most extraordinary feeling in my stomach. I'm back in the apartment now. Everyone's still asleep.

I think I had dropped off when the door opened quietly and I felt breath on my face.

'Can you get up?' he said. 'I need to talk to you.'

He waited for me in the kitchen while I got dressed and then we tiptoed out of the apartment and into the street. There was a pink tinge to the sky and the sound of a rubbish lorry churning several streets away.

William said, 'I just fancied some air. I needed to get out of there.'

'I know,' I said. 'It's weird.'

We walked, not talking, towards the river and took the bridge across from the island to the left bank. There's a ramp down to the river itself and we went down that, to a bench at the bottom. The Seine, mushroom brown, snaked past.

'Funny old night,' William said. 'Twelve hours of travelling and then this.'

I said, 'Poor Delilah. She was really looking forward to seeing you. She's been talking about you all the time.'

'Has she?'

'Yes,' I said.

'Look, Con, I want to talk to you about something.'

'Yes?'

There was a silence.

'I ... Con ... I ... We ... I mean ...' William stuttered.

'Huh?' I said.

'You know when ... ?'

'What?' I said.

'You know that day we ...'

'What?'

'You know.'

'Yes.'

'Well, did you ... ?'

'Did I ... ?'

'Did you, well ... oh, I don't know.'

He stared glumly ahead. Traffic was passing above us, but you couldn't see it. There was a high creamy wall between us and the city. I thought about what Julie had said about how complicated relationships are. About how we had to talk this one through. I felt so emotional suddenly I wanted to cry.

'William?'

He looked at me. His face was pale, his lips dry. The bench was cold under my legs.

I kissed him.

I know Julie's usually right. But not always.

We kissed for a long time.

I think before I'd been worried that being friends would make it tame, but it didn't. It wasn't embarrassing like that time on the sofa at home. I wasn't expecting it then. This time, it was so much better because I'd been waiting for it and thinking it was never going to happen. It felt dangerous and illicit and, well, delicious. We stopped kissing and hugged. He said, 'I only came to Paris to see you.'

'I only came to Paris to forget you,' I said.

We kissed some more. I didn't think about Philippe – I'd forgotten him long ago. And I don't think William thought about Delilah. Not for a while, anyway.

I was the one who said her name first. I broke off and said, 'What about Delilah?' I didn't hear his answer at first because it was muffled into my neck. (Oh, I do like being kissed on the neck.) I pulled away and looked at him. His eyes were on my mouth. He said, 'I do feel bad, but . . .' and I knew what he meant.

I said, 'What about our friendship?' and he said,

'Bugger our friendship!' and kissed me again.

On the walk back he said he's going to talk to Delilah today. 'It's not fair otherwise,' he said. 'Let her have her chance with Philippe.'

I told him about my lunch with Mother. We arranged to meet after it.

'Where do you want to go?' he said, as we reached the apartment. 'Let's go somewhere special.'

'The Eiffel Tower!' I said. 'I'll meet you there at four.'

At the door to Mimi's room, he said, 'I like your hair and your clothes, but I prefer the normal Connie.'

'You mean, the weird Connie.'

'The normal, weird Connie.'

He looked into my eyes. 'See you later, my normal, weird Connie. If you change your mind and don't come,' he said, 'I'll understand.'

SWOON.

Chapter Twenty-four

New vocab: *c'est sans espoir* (all hope is lost)

❤ *Mimi's living room, 11 a.m.*

I woke up twenty minutes ago, and remembered immediately about William. It was hard having breakfast with the others and pretending nothing had happened. Delilah was bossing him around in her usual princess way. He'd already been out to get croissants, but he hadn't got pain au chocolat. 'Baby, I always have a choccy croissant,' she said in her best little-girl voice. 'Plee-ease. Could you just nip out again?' He went, without looking at me. I think he was quite relieved to leave the apartment. When we meet up later at the Eiffel Tower he'll be a free man. Or a free fifteen-year-old boy at least.

I still can't believe it happened. Do I feel guilty? I don't think I do. I feel so tired, like I've been crying all night – which of course I haven't been. I would have felt guilty if it hadn't been for Delilah snogging Philippe. But I don't want D to be cross – and she will be, won't she? It'll be awkward for one thing, what with her living next door.

But I mustn't think about any of this now. I have to concentrate on the job in hand. I've rung my grandparents and fine-tuned the details. At 1 p.m. I'm meeting Mother and Mr Spence, and at 1.30 p.m. my grandparents are joining us. I still have to get washed and dressed – and get the food stain out of the plum top.

❤ *Pompidou top-floor restaurant, 1.10 p.m.*

I'm here. Alone. I'm suddenly v. apprehensive. I wish Mother would get here. The restaurant is v. starchy and modern at the same time. It's like a cross between the poshest hotel you've ever been in and some sort of designer shop where the assistants sneer at you when you walk in because they know you can't afford a shoelace. The tablecloths are white and the waiters are all in black, but not serving black, sort of high-fashion black. When I arrived they all ignored me, so I asked one of them – a man with sideburns and a goatee – if I could sit down and he looked almost affronted.

Our table is in the middle, not by the window, which reminds me I haven't mentioned the one important fact, which is that the view is INCREDIBLE. Paris really is laid out at our feet. You can see everything: the bleached buildings; the grey tiled roofs; the river, twinkling; the Sacré Cœur, like a white mosque on the hill there – all in a spring haze. Ha! And there's the Eiffel Tower, where, in less than three hours, I'll be meeting William for the most romantic afternoon of my life . . .

Why hasn't Mother got here yet? I'm getting very anxious. I've changed seats so I can see the entrance. You come up by escalator and then the last bit by lift and then you walk across a sort of gangplank into the restaurant. Mother should be here any second now. It's much better that she and Mr S should get here first – Julie's right. I'll have the chance to break it to her gently.

Who's this? Oh no. They're early! MY GRAND-PARENTS.

❤ *Mother's hotel, 4.15 p.m.*

This is the first moment I have had to write in here since the above. It has all gone wrong. I don't know what to do.

Mother is in the bathroom. She has been in there for forty-five minutes. Before that she was in the restaurant's *toilettes* for one hour and thirty minutes.

I don't know what I thought I was doing. I thought I knew what was best for Mother. I thought she needed to pull herself together, that it would all be wonderful, that she and her parents would fall into each other's arms and the last fifteen years would crumble away. I thought she'd snap out of her bad mood and forgive them. But it seems fifteen years isn't simply fifteen years – it isn't merely time. It's layer upon layer of stuff. Just after we got back here and before she locked herself in the loo, she said, 'It's not that simple, Constance. It's not just kiss and make up.'

I thought it was. I don't understand. And I suppose that's how it should be. It was thinking I understood that got me into this mess.

I can't blame my grandparents for getting there early. They thought she would be there at 1 p.m. They didn't know she was going to be delayed in a little jewellery shop in the Marais. I'd said 1.30 p.m. but their taxi was early and they were dying of excitement. My grand-mother was wearing the little blue suit I'd seen her eyeing in that shop the first day I saw her. My grand-father was carrying a newspaper. I had time, somehow, to notice the oddity of that – as if he was going to have time to read a paper with his long-lost daughter to fall upon.

They kissed me. My grandfather was waving the menu around with his spare hand, ordering champagne, and my grandmother was worrying about where to sit – who should sit with their back to the view, etc. – when I saw Mother and Mr Spence crossing the gangplank. I pushed my chair back – it was one of those high-fashion modern ones that looks like Playmobil – and knocked into one of the snooty waiter's heels. A vital second's delay was spent apologizing, by which point Mother was coming towards us. This is what happened to her face between the door and the table: 1) Expectant pleasure. 2) Mild bafflement. 3) Confusion. 4) Fury. When she reached stage four, she turned on her heels and ran, straight past the coat check and into the loos.

Mr Spence gave a cartoon wince, stretching his mouth apart like Wallace of Wallace and Gromit, and followed her. I stood, like a lemon. I didn't know what to do. The worst I'd imagined was shock and anger, that she'd shout at them, or maybe me, but that we'd thrash it out and everything would be all right. But, to be honest, what I'd really expected was total joy – hearts brimming, eyes filling – not, at any rate, a locked lavatory door.

My grandmother looked very small and frail. She cast her eyes from me to my grandfather as if expecting one of us to come up with the answer.

I said, 'I don't know.'

I sat back down. My grandmother's eyes were filling with tears. My grandfather had put his folded newspaper on the table and appeared to be reading a corner of it.

'I'll go and see what's happening,' I said.

Everyone seemed to be looking at me as I crossed the room past the other diners to the loos. They were impossibly modern. You could see the kitchen from them, which was a bit weird. Mother was in a cubicle with the door locked. Mr Spence was cross-legged on the floor outside. 'Come on now,' he was saying. 'There, there now. Come on now. There, there now.'

It was all awful. It went on for an hour and thirty

minutes. Mr Spence repeating himself over and over again. If I'd been Mother I'd have come out just to shut him up.

I tried to talk to Mother through the door. I kept saying how sorry I was to have shocked her, how much her parents loved her and had missed her and how desolated they were that she wouldn't come out. Mr Spence broke off his litany to say, 'Connie, I think maybe this was a mistake. Don't want to upset you, but didn't you think this might happen?'

'No, of course I didn't think this might happen, you cretin.'

Didn't say that, of course. I said, 'I know, you're right. It's a disaster.'

'There, there now. Come on now. There, there now,' he said.

My grandmother came and stood a few feet away. I hope when I'm a mother myself (if I ever am, urgh) I will have the courage to storm into a room if my kids are upset, to cover them with kisses and submerge them in hugs. That's all I ever want when I'm in a bad mood, even if I'm pretending to be all self-sufficient and cool. But my grandmother didn't do that. She stood back and watched. Then she turned and went back to the table where my grandfather continued to read the newspaper. I began to see how the family rift might have happened in the first place.

After one hour and fifteen minutes, the snooty waiters started getting even snootier. They had long given up on serving us, though they did deliver the bucket of champagne, which sat, undrunk, on our table. At 3 p.m. they told us we needed to leave, as we were disturbing other diners. We had actually been quiet, but it's true a queue had started forming for the one remaining lavatory, and the top of the Pompidou is simply not the sort of place to lower itself to queues.

Mr Spence got up off the lavatory floor and said, through the door, 'Bernadette, if you come out now, I will make sure your parents are nowhere near. I'll take you down to the street and into a taxi and back to our hotel. But we do need to leave now. I'm going to count to three.' He gestured to me to go back to the table – which, unwillingly, I did. I waited a few moments, stroking my grandmother's bony hand, and then I went back to see what was happening. The loo door was unlocked and they'd gone.

'It's ridiculous,' my grandmother said as we took the lift down to ground level. She had pulled herself together. 'It is so childish. It is *typique* of Bernadette. And that man with her . . . urgh.' I had been feeling really sorry for her, but this made me cross. I know Mr Spence is a geek, but I realize now that he's *our* geek.

'He's all right,' I said. 'He's good for her.'

'So, why did he take her away? From her own parents? He should have forced her to see us. I mean, what is this stubbornness about?'

I said I didn't know. They went home – I promised to ring them later – and I got the metro back to Mother's hotel. She was sitting in the bedroom, crying into Mr Spence's shoulder, when I arrived. We did begin to talk, but then she got all emotional and angry again and within seconds she was locked in the loo. Mr Spence has gone to get a sandwich. 'When a man's got to eat, a man's got to eat,' he said. I wish Mother would come out and cheer up. It's all too grown-up for me. I should stick with my own life. With school and my friends and William.

OH MY GOD.

WILLIAM!

♥ RER, 6.20 p.m.

I've ruined everything. I've ruined Mother's weekend. I've ruined my grandparents' old age by bringing them hope and dashing it. And now I've ruined any chance of happiness I might have had.

I am doomed to a life of loneliness and despair. I will be one of those mad cat-women with a house full of moggies, stinking of cat food and old newspapers.

I had completely and utterly and totally forgotten William.

Does this mean I don't love him? Or maybe it just means that until a certain age parents still come first.

I don't know where he is. Or what he is thinking. His last words to me last night were if I didn't come he'd understand.

After the shock of remembering, I yelled to Mother

through the bathroom door that I had to go out, that I wasn't deserting her, but I had something I'd forgotten to do – and fled from the hotel room. I asked the man at the desk and ran to the nearest metro. Then I ran, through all the Sunday tourists and all the tourist tack – the people selling battery-operated novelty toys and miniature Eiffel Towers on key rings – to the base of the tower. I didn't take much in – just the great steel legs and the entrance to the lift where we'd arranged to meet. It was 5.45 p.m. when I got there. I stood, people jostling around me, feeling lost. Then suddenly I saw a boy over to the left with his back to me. He was wearing a back-pack and jeans that trailed over the heels of his shoes. He was talking to a group of other boys, one shoulder slightly raised. The hair was the same, and the height. I started towards him, but then he turned and I realized what I'd known already, that it wasn't William.

All the trauma of the day and the sleeplessness of the night caught me up and I sat down where I was and cried for a bit. I was on my own in the middle of Paris. I had promised the Blancs that I would be home for supper. I was miles from La Varenne. Mother was still weeping in her hotel room. William was somewhere without me, convinced I'd changed my mind. Maybe he'd even gone back to Delilah. My grandparents are devastated. It is all a mess. I didn't know what to do. Go back to Mother's hotel? Go to Delilah's? Or my grandparents? Or go back to the Blancs?

In a daze, I got back to the metro and found the right

platform. Here I am now, shunting along on the RER, late back to the Blancs, probably in trouble. I have no idea what will meet me there. Will Monsieur Blanc have drunk himself into oblivion? Will Pascale have made it up with Eric? Will Didier still be speaking to me after the near-kiss of last night? Am I going to be in the most abysmal trouble for being so late? Will anyone have noticed?

I'm going home tomorrow.

I've achieved nothing.

I haven't even been up the Eiffel Tower.

Outside the window the suburbs look grey, not silver.

❤ *RER, 6.40 p.m.*

Oh, Lordy. I thought things couldn't get worse. I've just realized the Crying Girl is perched on the next seat along. Except she's not crying.

And I am.

❤ *P's bedroom, 8 p.m.*

I walked up the street to the Blancs' house earlier, convinced I was in trouble for being late. But when I reached the front door and rang the bell, no one came to answer it. I could hear voices — and laughter — not far away. I sat on the step and waited.

After about ten minutes the door opened and Pascale

came out. She said, 'Oh,' when she saw me, as if she'd forgotten I existed. Her hair was freshly washed and she was wearing jeans and a plain white T-shirt. She didn't have her heavy pan of make-up all over her face and her lips weren't black, but pink. There was pink in her cheeks too. There was something about her – I know, she looked fourteen.

She grinned. 'Constance! You're back!'

I felt as if I'd been gone for thirty-two years, not thirty-two hours.

'Come in. We're in the garden.'

I wanted to go upstairs, to lie on my bed. But I followed her through the living room – past the dining table, which was laden with dirty plates and glasses and the remnants of a meal – and out to the garden.

They were sitting at the table, drinking coffee: Didier, who gave me a formal salute as if our relationship was henceforth to be run on military lines; Philippe, who said 'hi' without looking at me; Monsieur Blanc, who got to his feet and brought out another cup and a dining chair for me to sit on; and, yes . . . Madame Blanc.

Later, Pascale told me her mother had come straight home the moment she received Didier's letter. The tears of her daughter, the pleading of her sons, the desperation of her husband had done nothing. News that her sister-in-law was rearranging her kitchen cupboards, on the other hand, had her back at home within minutes.

Madame Blanc smiled and handed me something. It

was a chocolate rabbit wrapped in cellophane. An Easter bunny. It was the first time I'd remembered it was Easter Sunday.

'Constance,' she said. 'We were worried about you.'

I wanted to say, we'd been worried about her, but I just smiled and thanked her for the rabbit. I could tell everything was OK. Philippe was clowning around as usual. Monsieur Blanc kept emitting short, loud barks of laughter, like a seal. Madame Blanc sat in their midst, Didier's arm round the back of her chair. Her hair was loose, which made her look younger. She was the queen bee back in her hive, her family around her. She looked happy and relieved. She wasn't, interestingly, wearing her apron.

She asked if I'd had supper and I said I hadn't. (Come to think of it, I hadn't even had lunch. Or breakfast.) She stood up as if she was about to get me something. Monsieur Blanc told her to sit back down, and that he would get it. I said, 'No, no. It's fine. I'm not very hungry,' and I had to force him to sit down again. The times, as some old pop geezer once said, they are a-changing.

It was getting dark and you could see the wind ruffling the flag on the roof of the house in the next street. But it wasn't cold. Those evergreens are like a wall, they keep the rest of the world out.

I sat there with them, but after a bit, I found I couldn't keep up with what they were saying. I was so exhausted all my French deserted me and it wasn't words I was

hearing but a stream of noise. I got up and said I was
turning in, but none of them really seemed to notice.

I looked out of the window when I got upstairs, and
they were all still out there in the dark, bundled round
the table, chatting and laughing together like a . . . well,
like a family.

You could say this diary has a happy ending after all.

Chapter Twenty-five

New vocab: *à bientôt* (see you soon)

Monday 14 April
💜 *P's bedroom,* 10 *a.m.*

I'm leaving in a few minutes. I'm packed and I've walked around the house to check nothing's left behind.

Pascale is taking me to the Gare du Nord and we're meeting Monsieur Baker – oh, long time no see, Monsieur Baker – at Passport Control. He left a message with Madame Blanc that Julie and I were not to go through without him. He said we needed an armed escort, or we'd end up in Luxembourg. It's not really fair. Left to my own devices, I'd never end up in Luxembourg. That's Julie's job, thanks v. much.

I've already said most of my goodbyes. Philippe, Didier and Madame Blanc went out to the *supermarché* half an hour ago. Philippe gave me a big hug and tried to slip his tongue into my mouth at the same time. I swatted him off like a fly, Lord love him. He's just not boyfriend material. I felt sadder saying goodbye to Didier. He was a kind friend to me while I was here. He said, '*Au revoir, la Constance*,' and did a theatrical sweep of an imaginary hat and kissed my hand. I could tell he was still hurt because he did that.

I never got a chance to say goodbye to Monsieur Blanc, just as I never really got to say hello, because he'd left for work before I got up. Madame Blanc kissed me and shook my hand at the same time. I feel warmly disposed towards her, but I don't feel we ever really met.

My grandparents rang this morning to find out what train I was on. They're going to wave me goodbye, which I'm glad about. It was my grandmother who rang and she sounded clipped and more formal than before, as if the shutters were down. She began to say something about Bernadette, but I told her I thought it was best if we didn't discuss Mother. 'We'll keep our relationship separate,' I said. 'And then it won't matter.' I could tell she'd rather if I ganged up with her against Mother, but she agreed.

I have spoken to Mother too. She rang, briefly, last night from Mr Spence's mobile. It was a bad signal. They were on the Eurostar home, I think. She said she was sorry for having reacted so badly. She said she understood why I did what I did, but that I was only a child and that I should not try always to understand her. We both cried a bit and she told me she loved me and I told her I loved her. I wish I could see her. But it's not long now. Tonight I'll be in my own bed, with my own cat curled against me and my own brother and sister jumping on the covers.

No news from William. I rang Julie but she hadn't heard anything. 'How's he getting home?' she said. I told her he was getting the coach. She said, 'You'll see him some time in the new year then.'

Pascale is being sweet. She can't wait to come to London in the summer. She wants to have a wild time. I told her she'd chosen the wrong girl to have a wild time with and she gave me a funny look. 'Liar,' she said.

I've given her my brown trousers and top. She looks nice in anything that's not black and I don't need them any more. They were magic trousers but the magic wore off. Do you know something? They just weren't me.

Pascale's just come in, tapping her watch. We've got to go.

💜 *Gare du Nord, Eurostar, carriage seventeen, 11 a.m.*

So, it's all over. Or nearly is. We're still in the station, but we're on the train, Julie and I, and this time we're sitting with the others. Monsieur Baker, v. dashing (not) in a black beret, is keeping his evil eye on us. Stacey

Owens has got an enormous bag of those madeleine cakes and is passing them around. Joseph Milton's got some Haribos. Good to know he's been absorbing the culture. It's all v. noisy. Everyone's got stories to tell. Julie's telling the whole gang how for the first few days she thought she was being poisoned. Abby Morton went skiing and broke her arm. There's a queue to scribble on her cast.

I cried saying goodbye to Pascale. We hugged each other downstairs, at the escalator. Eric was meeting her outside on his bike and taking her to the park. She looks so much happier than she did when I arrived. When her mother left them for those few days, Pascale found out how much her father loved her. Good things do sometimes come out of bad. I watched her as she left the station and walked into the sunshine. She is wearing black again today, but it looked purple in the light.

My grandparents were waiting for me upstairs; and my grandmother held my face to kiss me. She was smiling and looked much less tense.

'Bernadette rang us late last night,' she said. 'She gave us her apologies for her rudeness at lunch. She says she was not quite ready to see us, but maybe in a month or two, we would like to come to London to visit her — to visit you all.' There were tears in her eyes.

'I'm so glad,' I said. 'I really am.'

And I really am, but do you know? It doesn't seem so important now. The family that matters is the one waiting for me at home: Mother and Mr Spence, Marie and Cyril. And my head was still full of William.

Julie bundled up before they left.

'*Enchantée*, I'm sure,' she said cheekily when I introduced her.

'GIRLS!' squawked a panicked Monsieur Baker. 'Move it!'

So, that was that.

I'm glad I'm going to see them again soon. I'm glad my grandfather said, '*Enchanté*,' and kissed her hand. It shows he's got gallantry and a sense of humour. And next time — because now there is going to be a next time — I might get to see more of both.

❤ *Eurostar, carriage seventeen, 11.32 a.m.*

We're pulling out of the station now. All I can see is tracks and overhead wires, and the backs of buildings covered in graffiti. A crane, high-rise flats, a station, houses, a park, tennis court, wasteland . . .

I never did get to go up the Eiffel Tower.

It's all quietened down in the carriage. Julie's gone to see if she can get two Cokes with the money she's got left. If she hasn't got enough, she'll get one and we'll share it. I'm going to read *Madame Bovary* in a minute. I've hardly read any of it. I think she's about to be unfaithful to her husband. Not with a driving instructor, though.

Now we're on our way, I am so excited to be going home. There are butterflies in my stomach. I can't wait to see London, to get to our street, to see our house, my family and to be in my own room. I've missed the messiness of London, the ugliness, that combination of the smart and the tatty – you don't find that in Paris. You know, the ruched curtains in one house, the burnt-out car outside the next. And I've missed knowing the area where I live like the back of my hand; it's worth a lot, that. Everything's full of memories. I always said Paris was my spiritual home, but sometimes you have to go away to appreciate what you've got.

Julie's back (one Coke and a KitKat to share).

She's just said something odd.

'I thought William was getting the coach,' she said.

'He is.'

'Funny that. I've just met him in the buffet.'

💚 Eurostar, the buffet, 11.51 a.m.

It isn't far – only two carriages. I got here as fast as I could. He was leaning against the counter, drinking a cup of tea. When he saw me, he grinned and threw something in the air.

'You're late,' he said.

It was an Eiffel Tower key ring.

I only just caught it in time.